PRA...

JACK DASH AND THE
MAGIC FEATHER

'Arf arf arf arf ARF arf arf ARF!
(Scabby earlobes, this book is AMAZING. Don't be a
scaredy sock and read it NOW.)'
Opi, aged 10

'Original, brilliant and as funny as a pig on stilts!
Jack Dash is my kind of hero.'
Matt Brown, author of *Compton Valance*

'There's mayhem, there's madness, there's even a pet
sea lion! The world of Jack Dash is great fun!'
Ruth Fitzgerald, author of *Emily Sparkes*

'Thoroughly entertaining, exciting, funny and
imaginative - and I love the use of language
and place names. Brilliant!!'
Giles Andreae, author of *Billy Bonkers*

'It is funny with a capital 'F'!
Jack Dash and the Magic Feather is a crazy, clever
carnival ride of a story. Bonkers, brilliant and
feather-tastic! You had me at "Oi! Dozy Knickers!".'
Mo O'Hara, author of *My Big Fat Zombie Goldfish*

JACK DASH
AND THE
GREAT CUSTARD
CAKE-OFF

By
SOPHIE PLOWDEN

Illustrated by
Judy Brown

Catnip
PUBLISHING LTD

CATNIP BOOKS
Published by Catnip Publishing Ltd
320 City Road
London
EC1V 2NZ

This edition first published 2018
10 9 8 7 6 5 4 3 2 1

ISBN 978-1-910611-16-6

www.catnippublishing.co.uk

'If you climb in the saddle, get ready for the ride.'

Cowboy proverb

ONE

'Wozzat?'

Jack Dash felt something brush against his cheek. He opened his eyes: white fluffy somethings were swirling all around him, bouncing off his earlobes and landing on his pillow.

'Pppfffft!'

He wiped his mouth with the back of his hand. *It's the first day of the summer holidays* . . . he thought. *And it's snowing inside my bedroom . . . How's that even possible?* And then he remembered the blizzard – it was just a few weeks ago now – that had buried his school in a metre of snow and almost blown the roof off.

Jack sat up. *The weather's gone wonky again . . . that can only mean one thing. Someone's taken my magic feather!* He peered through the falling flakes at the small dark figure on the end of his bed. 'Pablo?'

The penguin pulled his head out from under the duvet: there were more fluffy somethings sticking to his beak and tumbling down his tummy. 'Hukka-hukka-hukka!' He flapped his wings, plunged his head back inside and pulled out a wad of stuffing.

'Hold on a half sec,' said Jack. 'It's not snowing at all. You've ripped up my duvet, you black and white basket case!' He scanned his bedroom floor and swallowed. 'And you've pooped all over my rug.'

'Haark!' Pablo scrabbled up the bed and pecked Jack on the cheek.

'Ouch!' he yelped. 'How many times do I have to –'

'Yoo–hoo!'

Jack froze. He felt his mouth go dry. 'Who's that?' he whispered.

Pablo shrugged his wings.

'Must be my mum. She'll be coming up the stairs! She'll snap her cracker if she finds a penguin in my bedroom.' In a flurry of fluff, Jack flung back his duvet and leaped out of bed. 'Quick! Quick! Where's your disguise?'

Jack fell to his knees and scrabbled through the heap of clothes on the floor: a trainer . . . a T-shirt . . . a dirty sock . . . A-ha! He pulled out a brown paper bag from under his jeans. He slipped Pablo's head through the slit in the bottom and smoothed it over his tummy. He snatched up a pair of rubber gloves, and one by one, he rolled them up Pablo's wings.

'Haark!' shrieked Pablo, flapping them in the air.

'Keep still, will you?' Jack seized a plastic flowerpot, with a fluffy green pom-pom glued to the top, and rammed it on Pablo's head. 'Perfect,' he said. 'And don't forget the rules. No flapping. No squawking. No pecking. No pooping. You've got to be on your best behaviour. You're s'posed to be a Swedish boy, remember?'

'Yoo-hoo!' the voice called again. And – *clack!* Something hard hit the window. 'Jack, you dumb-bum – are you there?'

'Huh?' Jack blinked. 'That's not my mum. It's that ginger-headed crack-pot,

Coco McBean.' He dragged a chair to the window; up he climbed and slid it open. Yep — it was Coco all right. She was leaning out of her bedroom window from the house next door. He could see her freckled hand waving from behind a TV aerial.

'Wakey-wakey, dozy-knickers!'

'What d'you do that for, you fruitcake?' said Jack. 'You almost gave me a heart spasm.'

'You're not gonna believe this.' She was pointing over Quarantine Street, across the rooftops of Curtly Ambrose to the very edge of the town. 'Look – over there! D'you see it?'

Gripping the windowsill, Jack raised himself on to his tiptoes and squinted into the distance. Yes! He could see something flashing silver in the sunlight, circling over the turrets of Castle Custard.

'Oh, this is so exciting!' said Coco. 'Bet you it's a private jet with a celebrity on board.'

'Too slow,' said Jack. 'The average

cruising speed of small jet is four hundred miles an hour.'

'Must be a helicopter then. Celebrities are always travelling in helicopters.'

Jack shook his head. 'Wrong shape. And there aren't any rotor blades.'

'OK, smartypants – what is it?'

Jack leaned out further, shielding his eyes with his hand. *Maybe it's a drone,* he thought, *except it's much too big. Or maybe . . . just maybe . . .* His heart began to flutter. 'D'you know something, Coco? I . . . I reckon it's a UFO.'

Coco clapped her hands. 'Yippee!' she cried. 'I love UFOs!' She pointed to a strip of white, which was stretched across the sky. 'And what's that thing behind it?'

'It looks like a banner . . . with writing on it.' Jack shivered. 'It must be some sort of alien message.'

'Really? Are you *sure*?' She screwed her eyes up and frowned. 'That's annoying. I can't see what it says.'

There are extra-terrestrials in Curtly Ambrose, Jack thought, *and they're actually trying to make contact.* His palms were sweating, his spine was tingling and his brain had started to boggle. 'We need to find out what they want. They've travelled hundreds of thousands of light years, Coco – it's gotta be something important.' He scratched his head. *Think, think, think!* He heard a rustle behind him: Pablo was shuffling over with a long golden feather clamped in his beak.

Of course! Jack jumped off the chair with a thud.

'Hey!' yelled Coco. 'Where are you going?'

Jack sat down at the rickety desk, which was tucked in the corner of his bedroom. He lifted out his ancient book and opened its green leather cover. He reached out his hand. 'OK, Pablo – pass me the feather!' And he plucked it from Pablo's beak.

I can draw anything. Jack twirled the feather between his fingers: it glistened like gold and crackled like fire. He stroked its shimmering fronds and tapped its tip, which was sharpened and stained with ink. *Anything I want and – zap! It'll come to life.* He looked at Pablo and grinned.

'I know!' he said. 'I'm gonna draw a high-res, long-distance, digital telescope.'

Pablo cocked his head.

'What are you looking at me like that for? It's a great idea! I'll be able to zoom right in and read that message like it was right here in this room. Oh, wow!' Jack's heart was pounding now. 'What if it's some sort of invitation like . . . like an alien birthday party?'

'Hrrf!' Pablo shook his head.

'You're right.' Jack felt his heart slump. 'It's probably written in Alienese and we won't be able to read it. Hmm . . . we're gonna have to get their attention somehow.' He frowned and scratched his eyebrow. 'I know − I'll draw a massive flag and wave it out of the window.'

'Haark!' Pablo widened his eyes − his

feathers were standing on end.

'OK, OK. That's a bad idea. What if they're planning a hostile takeover?' Jack bit his lip. 'Things could turn very nasty. They might fly their spaceship over here and atomise the street.' He looked at Pablo and gulped. 'This could be the start of an intergalactic war!'

'HAARK!' screeched Pablo, and buried his head in his wings.

'S'OK,' said Jack. 'I'll protect you. I'm gonna draw a ray gun, just in case.' He took a deep breath and closed his eyes for a moment, then he pressed the feather tip to the paper. In a thin black line, he guided it over the page. *Keep going, keep going, keep going.* With a sweep of his wrist he made a loop. 'That's the handle . . .' he said, 'and this is the blaster.' And he added a shape like a cone.

'Huk! Huk-huk!' squawked Pablo, hopping from foot to foot.

'Hold on! I haven't finished yet.' He sketched three little circles in a row. 'They're the control buttons, see? The first one's *Start*, the next one's *Stop* and the one at the end is for *Extra-Mega-Boost*.'

'Hukka-hukka-hukka!' Pablo flapped his rubber gloves. He was pointing his beak at the door.

'Don't worry,' said Jack. 'I've got it all sorted. One false move and – **zigga-zagga-zam** – I'll shoot their spaceship out of the sky and into the Milky Way!'

'Dumpling?'

Mum! She was standing in the doorway of his bedroom. Jack whisked the feather into his desk and slammed the lid shut.

'Time to get up. Breakfast's ready.' She looked at the floor, then across at his bed. Her lip began to wobble. 'Goodness me, what a *dreadful* mess! What's happened to your duvet?'

Gotta get her out of here fast, thought Jack. *Any second now and – zap! The ray gun will come to life.* 'It . . . er . . . got a bit hot, that's all. It must've exploded in the middle of the night.'

'Huk-huk-huk!' Pablo nodded his head.

'Oh dear!' said Mum, tottering backwards. 'That doesn't sound very safe.'

'Come on!' Jack leaped to his feet and hurried her out through the door. 'We better evacuate immediately, in case there's a secondary eruption.'

two

'I've got some terribly exciting news.' Mrs Dash put down her teacup and beamed. 'I bet you can't guess what it is!'

Jack stopped chewing. His toast went limp in his hand. *I bet I can,* he thought. *She's booked me in for ballet lessons again.*

Mum giggled. 'I've entered the Curtly Ambrose Cake-Off Competition, and I'm through to the first round!'

'Huk-huk!' went Pablo, bouncing up and down in his high chair.

'I know, I know,' she said, dabbing at her eyes. 'I can't believe it's true! Just think – this could be the start of a new career: biscuits in Asbo's . . . a chain of restaurants . . . The Dottie Dash Show on TV . . .' She clasped her hands together and shivered. 'Oh, I'm ever so excited – with just a *teeny* sprinkling of nerves!'

Pablo stood up on his seat and – 'Hukka-hukka-hukka!' – he slapped his rubber gloves together.

Dad sighed from behind his newspaper. 'Is that Swedish boy still here?'

Pablo, please! thought Jack. *Act like a human and don't do anything weird!*

'Oh, I know it won't be easy,' said Mum. 'I'm up against Dr Spleen. That's *the* Dr Spleen. The Cake-Off Champion. He's won it eight years in a row.'

Pablo squawked. His beak fell open.

Time to take him upstairs, Jack thought, chewing his toast double-quick. *My ray gun must be ready by now. We'll check on the aliens and – Uh-oh!* Dad was lowering his paper.

'I thought he was supposed to be learning English.' Mr Dash peered over his glasses and frowned at Pablo. 'It's been six weeks! Six whole weeks and he hasn't learned a single word.'

'He's trying his hardest, aren't you, Pablo?' Mrs Dash patted Pablo's pompom and smiled. 'Now eat your breakfast like a good little boy.'

Splat! Pablo plunged his face into his bowl of cornflakes.

'I've had enough of this,' said Dad. 'Why can't he use a spoon, like everybody else?' He picked one up from the table and tapped Pablo's bowl with a **clink-clink-clink**. 'Spoon,' he said. 'Sp – *oooo* – n.'

Pablo lifted his head from the bowl,

milk dripping down his neck. He looked at Dad and burped.

Jack gulped. *Oh, no! I've gotta get him outta here!*

Mr Dash was wagging his finger in front of Pablo's face. 'Naughty Pablo! Very rude!'

Pablo twitched. He narrowed his eyes.

'No!' Jack yelped. 'Stop!' His parents were staring at him now. 'He . . . er . . . he can't use a spoon – he doesn't know how – they don't have spoons in Sweden, you see. It's so cold their fingers get stuck to the metal.'

'Don't have *spoons*?' said Mum. 'How do they stir their soup?' She checked her watch. 'Goodness me!' She pushed back her chair and jumped to her feet. 'Nine o'clock, already – the Cake-Off starts at ten and I've got a thousand and one things to do.' She flung the kitchen cupboard open, piling boxes into her arms. 'Now, where did I put my oats?'

Cock-a-doodle doo!

Phew! thought Jack. *The doorbell!* 'I'll get that!' He scooped Pablo out of his high chair and hauled him into the hall. He turned the handle and – BAM! The front door flew open.

The Fruitcake was standing on the doorstep, with her backpack in her arms.

'Guess what I've got in here?'

'Not now, Coco – I don't have time. Hostile aliens are planning an invasion –

I've gotta go upstairs and sort them out.'

'It's a Penguin Survival Kit. I got it off eBay.' She pulled back the flap and peered inside. 'Toenail clippers . . . Krunchy Krill bars . . .' She pulled out a large blue packet and dumped it on the floor. 'Ta-dah! A packet of Penguin Poop Deodoriser Granules.'

'Listen,' Jack hissed. 'Cut the penguin talk, will you? Mum and Dad are in the kitchen and –'

'Hello, Coco!' said Mrs Dash, as she bustled into the hall. 'Have you heard the news?' She gave a shiver. 'I'm doing the Cake-Off!'

Coco frowned. She twizzled her pigtail. She stared at the tangle of shiny tubing lying on Jack's bedroom floor. It was more than a metre long, looping and twisting over itself, and flaring out at one end. 'Erm . . . What's it s'posed to be?'

Jack sighed and rolled his eyes. 'It's a ray gun, you triple-baked tortoise.'

'O-*kaaay*.' She folded her arms and nodded slowly. 'I never knew ray guns were as big as that. Are you sure you drew it right?'

''Course I did. Everyone knows that ray guns are massive. It's how they generate power.' He pointed to the window. 'Do me a favour, will you? Keep an eye on the spaceship and if you see anything funny, anything at all, then – Hey!' he cried. 'What d'you think you're doing?'

'That's weird.' Coco was kneeling on the floor, peering into the blaster. 'I can't see any rays.'

'That's 'cos they're invisible, you fruitcake. Now, leave it alone. It's a highly sophisticated weapon with the capability to wipe out an entire solar system in one lethal blast, and it could go off any –'

CLANG! Pablo staggered sideways as she rapped it with her knuckles. 'You'll never guess what . . .' She picked it up and poked her finger inside. 'I think it's made of brass.'

'S-stop!' Jack squeaked. 'I'm being s-serious, Coco – put it down! The rays could shoot out any moment.'

'Don't get your knickers in a noodle, I'm just trying to see how it works.' She twirled her freckled finger over the controls. 'So what do these buttons do?'

'NOOO!' Jack flung his arms over his head and crumpled to the floor. *This is it,* he thought. *She's gonna vaporize my vital organs and blast my bedroom to bits.*

What was that? He raised his elbow a millimetre and a half and peeked out from underneath: Pablo was skittering in circles over the floor, flapping his gloves and jerking his neck.

'Cool!' said Coco. She slid the handle forwards. 'It's got moving parts and everything!' She puffed out her cheeks and blew down the tube:

WOOOoooooaaAAARP!

'I knew it!' She turned to Jack and grinned. 'It's one of those bony-wotsits.'

Jack blinked. His could still feel the

echo bouncing round his skull. 'I . . . I dunno what you're on about, but you practically perforated my eardrum.'

'A trombone,' said Coco. 'That's the one.' She gave it one last tap and dumped it on the bed. 'Like a trumpet but weirder.'

I don't understand, he thought. *I drew a ray gun – I know I did.* He eased himself on to his knees. Something strange was happening: the more he looked at the ray gun, the less like a ray gun it looked. 'I've really messed up, big time,' he wailed. 'How are we gonna fight off the aliens now? We're completely and utterly defenceless! We're at the mercy of an army of cosmic beings! We're . . . *Coco?*' he said. 'Are you listening?'

She was sitting at his desk, with Pablo on

her knee. 'Hold on a sec – I'm trying to clip his toenails and it's actually quite fiddly.'

'*Please*,' he said. 'I need you to concentrate – this is vitally important. The future of Curtly Ambrose is at stake!'

'Huh?' She was peering at Pablo's webbed orange foot. 'Didn't quite catch that. What were you saying again?'

'Aliens!' he cried. 'I'm talking about the aliens at Castle Custard.'

'Oh, don't worry.' Coco popped Pablo back on to the floor and brushed the clippings off her lap. 'I reckon your mum'll sort them out.'

'My *mum*? What's my mum got to do with it?'

'Cos she's gone to Castle Custard, of

course.'

'Hold it,' said Jack. 'Hold it right there. Are you trying to tell me that the Curtly Ambrose Cake-Off Competition is taking place at Castle Custard?'

Coco beamed. 'Haven't you heard? They're filming it this year. She's gonna be on the telly!'

'What's wrong with you, you dizzy-headed dimwit? Why didn't you tell me this before?' Jack paced his bedroom floor, his mind spinning like a hamster in a wheel. 'This is bad,' he said. 'This is worse than bad – it's absolutely abysmal. My mum's in mortal danger – she could be abducted any moment.' He shuddered all over. 'They'll grab her with their little green fingers and bundle her into the hold.' He grabbed his scarf off the floor and wound it round his neck. 'OK, Coco – we need to get down there ASAP. We'll get the bus to the High Street and trek across the fields.'

Coco looked up from his desk and grinned. 'I've had a better idea.'

tHREE

'Coco?' said Jack. 'What have you just done?'

'Well . . .' She placed Jack's feather back on his desk, its fronds still fizzing with sparks of gold. 'You said you were in a hurry and you seemed a bit upset, so I thought I'd help you out, 'cos I'm really good at drawing.'

ZAP! BANG!

Pablo jumped back and gave a squawk.

And there it stood, in the middle of his bedroom: a metre-long plank on a set of little wheels. A mast rose from its centre, which almost touched the ceiling – it was tied with a large pale blue sail.

'Hukka-hukka-hukka!' Pablo bounced
up and down, flapping his rubber gloves.

'What . . .' said Jack, 'is *that*?'

'It's a three-person roller-board-sailing-buggy-thingy,' said Coco. 'I sort of made it up.'

'It's a multi-coloured monstrosity, more like. If you think I'm riding on that contraption, then you're out of your ginger mind.' He sighed and shook his head. 'Look at it, will you? It's an accident waiting to happen – there aren't any seat belts, for one thing, and you've forgotten to draw the headlights.'

'Everybody ready?' With the trombone hooked over her shoulder, Coco hopped on to the buggy. She turned around and frowned at Jack. 'You've got a sieve on your head.'

'Actually, it's an intergalactic alien-proof helmet, and I'm wearing it for protection.'

'If you say so.' She tugged at the rope.

Jack ducked to the left as the sail swung round. 'Watch what you're doing! You practically sliced my nose off.'

'Whoopsie! I think you'll have to budge up a bit.'

'And how am I s'posed to do that?' Jack squeaked, clinging to the mast with both hands. 'Pablo's standing on my foot, and one of your pigtails is halfway up my nose.' He peered over Coco's shoulder and down the stairs, to the landing below. 'It looks a bit steep to me. I hope you remembered to draw the airbags.'

'Relax,' she said, paddling forwards with her foot. 'Just hold on tight and don't forget to breathe.'

'Stop!' Jack whimpered. 'I've changed my mind. I want to get – AARGGH!' His tummy lurched into his throat as they *bump*

    – *bump*

        – *bump*ed down the stairs.

I knew

    – I knew it

        – I knew it, he thought. *She's flipped right out of her tangerine tree.*

Clackity-clack – he could hear the mast scraping the ceiling and the sail slapping the wall.

'Brace position!' yelled Coco.

KA-DUMP!

The buggy came to a halt on the landing.

'I – I think I've lost one of my kneecaps,' Jack gasped. 'And my spine's about to –'

'One more flight to go!' cried Coco, kicking off from the wall.

Bump, bump, bump – the sail buggy slammed down the stairs again.

We're gonna crash — we're gonna crash — we're gonna crash . . . Jack could see his father in the entrance hall below, gazing up, his mouth hanging open. 'Dad!' he bellowed. 'Open the door!'

FOUR

'We're taking the shortcut,' said Coco. She tugged at the rope and leaned into the wind, her pigtails flapping in Jack's face. The mast creaked. The sail billowed. The buggy clattered down Quarantine Street, its wheels jittering over the paving stones.

That doesn't sound right, thought Jack. *There's something wrong with the axle.* 'Coco?' he yelled. 'Stop the buggy – we've got a technical malfunction!'

'Chill out, chicken-knickers – everything's under control.' She gave the rope another tug and – *ka-dump!* it veered off the kerb.

'Look out!' Jack cried. 'Someone's crossing the –'

BOOMPH!

He glanced over his shoulder and gasped: a woman was sitting in the middle of the road, half a dozen eggs splattered around her, and her shopping bag lying in the gutter. 'Watch where you're going, you mango-coloured maniac – you practically ran her over.'

'Wa-hey!' Coco yanked the rope again: the sail swung and – *whoosh!* – they swerved around the corner into Vaccine Lane.

Jack heard a bark, and then he saw it: a pair of wild eyes . . . a jaw of jagged teeth . . . a ball of brown fur, was bounding beside the buggy, snapping at Pablo's tail feathers and trying to scramble on board.

'Haaark!' screeched Pablo.

'Hoist the spinnaker!' Jack cried. 'We're being attacked by a mutant poodle!'

'Yippee!' Coco kicked out her left leg

and jerked the buggy sideways.

Ka-dump! Up on to the kerb they lurched, their shadow whizzing over the pavement as the wheels thrummed beneath them. Coco was whooping above the buffeting wind.

'You can slow down now,' Jack called. 'I think we've shaken it off.'

Past Influenza Close they thundered, and into Shingles Road.

'Coco?' he yelled. 'We're going too fast.'

'Gotta catch those aliens, remember?'

Beeeeep! A car horn blasted.

Jack could hear someone shouting, and the **ting-ting-ting** of a bicycle bell. *Hope we get there soon, 'cos I'm about to lose* *my breakfast.* Gripping the mast in both hands, he clenched his eyes shut. The wind whipped his face, stinging his cheeks, his bones rattling like a box of broken toys.

Bump-rattle-bump – the buggy was slowing down at last.

Jack opened his eyes: they were out of Curtly Ambrose now, trundling down a country lane and through a tunnel of trees, joggling and jolting over the ruts. Into the sunlight they bounced, rolling green fields stretching ahead. *I need to make a plan,* he thought, *if I'm gonna outwit those aliens. We'll sneak inside, grab my mum and slip her out the back.*

Jack tilted back his head and scanned the skies for a silver spacecraft: clouds were scudding across the blue . . . birds crying in the wind . . . leaves looping and spinning in the air. Still no sign of the UFO. *They're probably hovering close to the ground, looking for a parking space.* He patted his intergalactic alien-proof helmet. *It's a good job I came prepared.*

FIVE

Coco yanked hard on the rope and dug her right heel into the ground. The sail sagged. The buggy skidded sideways and creaked to a halt.

'What are we stopping for?' said Jack. 'We're not even there yet.'

'There's a fence in the way, you dumb-plop – I need you to open the gate.' She pointed across the field. 'That's Castle Custard. D'you see it?'

Yes! There were the gleaming turrets, poking up through a clump of trees. Jack jumped off the buggy and swung the gate open. 'Come on, Coco – let's get moving.'

He tapped his foot and drummed his fingers on the fence. What was The Fruitcake doing? Why was she staring like that? 'Move it, will you? Once those aliens land, it's gonna be absolute mayhem.'

'In the field,' she hissed. 'Behind you!'

Jack turned round. His jaw fell open: a herd of hairy creatures – fifty . . . sixty . . . seventy or more – were advancing over the hill towards him. 'Um . . . maybe this wasn't such a good idea.'

'Wow,' she said. 'They're like walking bath mats. Giant bath mats. Look at the size of their horns!'

Jack backed out of the field, one slow step at a time. 'Don't make a sound,' he whispered. 'The smallest noise could set them off.' He clicked the gate shut and turned around. 'Where's Pablo?'

'Dunno,' said Coco. 'He was right beside me a second ago.'

'Oh no!' A small figure in a brown paper bag was scrambling under the fence. 'P-Pablo!' he yelled. 'Come back!'

Coco shrugged. 'Nope,' she said. 'He's not listening.'

'Hukka-hukka-hukka!' Pablo was standing in the middle of the field, waggling his rubber gloves at the beasts. He thrust his head forwards and stuck out his tongue.

'What's he teasing them for?' Jack cried. 'He must be out of his black and white mind!'

'That's strange,' said Coco. 'There's steam coming out of their nostrils.'

'They're closing in,' said Jack. 'He doesn't stand a chance. They'll flatten him into a penguin pancake and skewer his intestinal tract!'

'Don't worry.' She slid the trombone off her shoulder. 'I'll sort it.'

'Coco!' he wailed. 'No!' Jack slammed his hands to his ears as she raised it to her lips.

Pablo staggered backwards. Birds in their hundreds took to the sky, and fifty … sixty … seventy beasts or more, pricked up their ears, their noses twitching. One of them snorted and pawed at the ground.

'Whoopsie!' said Coco. 'I think they're gonna charge.'

'You idiot!' Jack cried. 'You twerp! You ginger-coloured clot-head!'

The earth trembled. The air thrummed with the pounding of hooves. Pablo flung himself on to his tummy as the creatures came thundering towards him, kicking and bucking and leaping.

'Wowza,' said Coco. 'I didn't know bath mats could move that fast.'

'Congratulations,' said Jack. 'You've started a stampede.' And what was that over there? He leaned over the fence: uh-oh! An old man in a hat was pounding down the field, waving a walking stick over his head.

'Hooligan!' the old man yelled. 'Vandal! Pipsqueak!' He rounded on Pablo, panting and wheezing. 'What d'you think you're playing at, eh? You've scared me yaks senseless!'

'Hrrf!' Pablo fluffed up his feathers.

'Don't you take that tone with me, young man. Those yaks are *extremely* sensitive. Very rare breed, dontcha know.'

He bent down and prodded Pablo's tummy. 'Any more of your shenanigans and I'll set the peacocks on you.'

Coco giggled. 'Here we go.' She pointed to a yak: head down and horns gleaming, charging towards the old man's bottom as fast as its hooves would carry it.

Jack held his breath.

'I'll have you tossed into the dungeons,' the old man was barking. 'I'll have you – AAAARGH!'

Jack looked at Pablo and gulped. The old man lay sprawled at their feet. He could hear the distant mooing of yaks as they scattered over the hill.

'Well?' called Coco from over the fence. 'Is he moving?'

'I – I dunno.' Jack knelt down. Grasping the old man's gnarled hand, he peered into his wizened face. 'I think his eyelid's twitching.'

'Thought so,' she said. 'He's fine. Come on, you two – we're s'posed to be hunting aliens.'

The old man's lips parted. He let out a moan.

'We can't leave him like this,' said Jack. 'He's had a serious injury. He's probably suffering from a chronic case of concussion.'

Coco sighed and clambered over the

fence. She plonked the trombone on the ground, bent over the old man and lifted up her pigtail. 'That's weird. I think he just said "turnip".'

Jack leaned in close – yes, he could hear the old man mumbling, too. '"Marrow" . . . I definitely heard him say "marrow".' He flapped his hand under the old man's nose. 'I think he needs more air.'

'How about I jump on his chest?' said Coco. 'Get his heartbeat going?'

'What are you trying to do?' Jack cried. 'Finish him off completely? This is one million per cent your fault, you know that? If you hadn't been messing around with that trombone this never would've happened.'

'OK,' said Coco. 'How about biscuits and a cup of sweet tea? My gran always says they work wonders.'

'Thanks for the handy tip. Except – maybe you hadn't noticed – we're in a field in the middle of nowhere. Where are we gonna find tea and biscuits?'

Coco shuffled off her backpack and plunged her arm inside. 'Easy,' she said, and handed Jack his feather.

'Hmm . . .' Coco leaned over Jack's shoulder. 'I s'pose it'll have to do.'

'What's the problem now?' said Jack. 'I drew a box of biscuits and a cup of tea just like you – hey!' he cried, as she whisked the feather out of his hand.

She gave the feather a shake and *splat* went the ink up the page. *Splat! Splat! Splat!*

'What are you *doing*?' said Jack.

'Adding sugar, of course.'

Jack plonked the notebook on the ground. 'Thanks a bunch, Coco – you've ruined it.'

ZAP! BANG!

'Haaark!' Pablo staggered backwards and flapped his rubber gloves.

'That's gotta be a world record,' said Coco. 'It's the biggest box of biscuits I've ever seen.'

Jack looked up at the box and gulped.

She's right, he thought. *It's absolutely ginormous.* He peeked round one side . . . then the other . . . He poked his head round the back. 'I don't get it. Where's the cup of tea?'

'What?' The old man sat up and blinked. 'Did someone mention tea?' He looked at Jack. 'And who the devil are you, with that tin pot on your head?'

Jack gulped. 'I'm –'

'Don't like the cut of your jib, sir. I'll have you clapped in irons.' He hauled himself to his feet and turned unsteadily to Pablo. 'And as for you, sir – you puffed-up popinjay – attacking me derrière with a bludgeon! I'll have you hung on a fence and left for the crows. Blinking crows . . . blasted nuisance. Woodpeckers too. Frightful things. *Tap! Tap! Tap!* All day long! Tease me yaks to distraction with their infernal racket.'

The old man tottered towards the box.

'Hello?' He scratched his head. 'When did they put this here, eh?' He stumbled round it, tapping at its sides with his stick. 'Aha! A door.'

A door? thought Jack. *I don't remember drawing a door.*

But the old man was pulling it open.

'Facilities too – just the ticket!' He picked up the trombone and heaved it over his shoulder. 'Mustn't forget me blunderbuss. Can't be too careful these days.' He swayed for a moment, then tottered inside and – *bam!* – slammed the door shut.

'Coco?' Jack whispered. 'What's that noise?'

'Sounds like he's whistling.'

Jack heard a flush. 'I don't get it. What's going on?'

Coco giggled. 'I think you drew a Port-a-Lav.'

Pablo nodded. 'Huk-huk-huk!'

Jack scratched his head. 'What exactly are you two on about?'

'You know,' said Coco. 'One of those portable toilets – there's one in the car park right behind Asbo's. My granny got stuck in it once when I jammed the lock with a lollipop stick.'

The box shuddered. Water was bubbling up from underneath and spreading over the ground.

'Get back!' Jack yelled. 'It's sprung a leak!' The box began to rattle. It was rocking to and fro, gurgling and hissing and spurting. 'This is your fault, Coco. You messed up my drawing.'

'HAARK!' screeched Pablo.

WHOOMPH!

The box took off on a blast of spray ten . . . twenty . . . thirty metres high.

Pablo's beak fell open.

Jack watched the box soar through the air, arcing over the treetops towards Curtly Ambrose, smaller and smaller, till it melted into the blue. 'It must be going a thousand miles an hour,' he breathed.

'Really?' said Coco. 'That's even faster than the Zombie Killer Water Ride at Barchester Towers.'

Jack rubbed his eyes with his fists. He looked down at the square of flattened grass, where the box had stood only seconds before.

'He's gone,' he murmured. 'Just like that.'

Coco patted his shoulder. 'Don't worry. He'll have a blast. Old people love those things. I took my gran on the Bouncing Boomerang Ride and –'

'Will you stop going on about your gran?' said Jack, raking his hand through his hair. 'This is serious, Coco – we've sent him into space in a portable toilet. He's orbiting the planet!'

'What's the problem? He's gotta come down sometime.'

Of course, thought Jack. *The force of gravity – she's making sense for once. Hmm* . . . He scratched his head. *One circuit of the globe at a thousand miles an hour . . . multiplied by twenty-four hours in a day . . . at an angle of trajectory of approximately sixty-eight degrees*

. . . He counted it out on his fingers. *Plus thirteen minutes for turbulence over the Matterhorn, just to be on the safe side* . . . 'OK,' he said. 'By my calculations, he should be landing outside the grocer's on the High Street at 10.17 tomorrow morning.'

'Get a move on, slug-bum!' Coco was standing on the buggy-board, tugging at the rope. 'We're ready to sail!'

SIX

The sail buggy clattered through the huge iron gates. At the end of the drive, Castle Custard rose from its shimmering moat, at the foot of a wooded hill; flags fluttered above the ramparts and a drawbridge led to a huge stone arch, studded with shields and crests. On the lawn beside it stood a big white tent, with a sign above the entrance saying: CURTLY AMBROSE CAKE-OFF. Peacocks were strutting on the grass. People with headsets and microphones were buzzing in and out.

'OK,' Jack called. 'Stop here.'

Coco tugged the rope and dug her heel

into the ground again, and the buggy shuddered to a halt between a row of parked cars.

'I can't see any aliens,' said Jack, peeking round the side of a big blue truck. 'They must've gone into hiding.'

'Look!' squealed Coco. 'They're filming!' She pointed to the marquee, where a blonde woman in a scarlet suit was standing by the entrance, talking to a man with a camera on his shoulder. 'That's Kelly-Ann Caraway off Curtly Ambrose TV!'

'Listen, Coco – I've made a plan. We'll start by . . . Coco?'

What was The Fruitcake doing?

Jack charged after her and pulled her back by the arm. 'How many times do I have to tell you? Stop messing about!'

'What's the problem now? I was only gonna ask for her autograph.'

Jack gripped her by the elbow. 'This is A-1 mega-grade serious – we've got to find my mum and get her out.'

'Okey dokey, let's start here.' She opened the tent flap. 'This looks exciting!'

The tent was blazing with lights inside. Cameras . . . cables . . . a large flat-screen TV . . . At one end sat the audience on rows of plastic chairs, and at the other end the contestants were running to and fro, sprinkling, rolling, chopping, opening fridges and slamming oven doors.

'Huk!' Pablo was jumping up and down, pointing with his beak. 'Huk-huk!'

'There she is,' said Coco. 'Right at the back – next to that man with the purple lips.'

Jack stood on his tiptoes and craned his neck: Mum was whisking a bowl at her baking station, wearing a blue frilly apron and her lilac tiara.

He took a deep breath. 'Ready, you two?' He dropped to his hands and knees and crawled into the tent, with Pablo beside him, scooting along on his tummy. 'Coco – you keep a lookout while I . . . *Coco?*'

He looked left. He looked right. 'Where's she gone now?'

An announcement came over the tannoy: *'THE FIRST ROUND OF THE CAKE-OFF WILL FINISH IN FIFTEEN MINUTES.'*

'We don't have time to find her,' said Jack. 'It's you and me, Pablo – we're going in.'

'A spaceship? Over Castle Custard?' Mrs Dash shook her head. 'I don't think so, Dumpling – not today. Now, go and sit down. You're not allowed in the baking area.'

'But – but I saw it!' Jack wailed. 'And I think they might be planning an intergalactic war!'

'Out of my way, sweetie!' Mrs Dash pulled on her padded gloves and opened the oven door. 'Goodness me!' She slid out a tray and laid it on the counter with a clatter. 'I'm *sure* I turned the oven on.'

'And there was a message,' said Jack. 'Right behind it – on a massive sign in the sky.'

Pablo nodded. 'Huk-huk-huk!'

'A sign . . .' said Mum, gazing at the soggy lump on her tray.

'Come on,' said Jack, tugging at her sleeve. 'It's not safe here. We've got to vacate the premises.'

'It's raw,' said Mum. 'Do you think it matters?'

'Mum, *please*! They've probably already landed. They could attack any moment.'

'Oh, I remember!' she said. 'This morning, there was one of those old-fashioned aeroplanes with a propeller on its nose.'

'An aeroplane?' said Jack. 'No, Mum – it was a UFO.'

'Buzz, buzz, buzz! Flying around like a bumblebee . . .' She looked at Jack and smiled. 'With a lovely big banner tied to its tail, saying "Welcome to the Cake-Off".'

'But . . . but . . .' Jack closed his eyes. He breathed in. He breathed out.

'Some people *like* uncooked cakes,'

he could hear her saying. 'In fact, they're rather French!'

So, it wasn't a spaceship after all! He could feel a laugh from deep within his tummy, bubbling up into his chest.

'Jack?' said his mum. 'Do stop snorting, and say hello to Dr Spleen. He's doing the Cake-Off too.'

A tall, dark man in a long white coat was leaning over her counter. He was wearing a stethoscope round his neck and a thin smile on his purple lips.

'We're safe!' Jack cried. He spluttered. He giggled. He punched the air. 'No more aliens! The invasion's over!'

The doctor raised an eyebrow. He looked Jack up and down.

'And . . . er – this is Pablo,' said Mum. 'He's from Sweden.'

'Hukka-hukka-hukka!' Pablo was jumping and flapping his rubber gloves.

'CONTESTANTS, YOU HAVE TEN MINUTES. WOULD THE JUDGE KINDLY MAKE HIS WAY TO THE PRESENTATION TABLE?'

'Now, come along, you two,' said Mum. 'Go and sit down!'

Jack leaned back in his chair and patted Pablo's glove. 'You can relax,' he said. 'It's like I always thought – it wasn't a spaceship after all.' He looked up at the flat-screen TV: Kelly-Ann Caraway was checking her watch and looking over her shoulder.

'WOULD THE JUDGE PLEASE COME TO THE PRESENTATION TABLE IMMEDIATELY?'

The audience began to murmur.

'Strange . . .' said the lady in front,

who was wearing a yellow straw hat. 'Why's Lord Crumble late?'

'I'm not surprised at all,' said the gentleman beside her. 'Very odd man. Never leaves his castle. Must get lonely in that gloomy old place. He's probably gone a bit dotty.'

'I spotted him in a field once,' somebody else was saying. 'Looked like a scarecrow.'

'Yaks, you know,' the gentleman replied. 'He's utterly obsessed with them. Some sort of rare breed, apparently.'

Jack went cold. 'Pablo?' he rasped. 'Did he say "yaks"?'

Pablo nodded slowly.

A thought was bouncing round Jack's

brain – a thought so terrible it made his tonsils tingle. 'P-Pablo?' he croaked. 'Are you thinking what I'm thinking?'

Pablo nodded again.

'What are we gonna do?'

Pablo looked at him and shivered. He buried his face in his gloves.

'*WE REGRET TO INFORM YOU THAT THE CAKE-OFF HAS BEEN DELAYED, UNTIL FURTHER ANNOUNCEMENTS.*'

A voice wailed from the baking area. Mum was clinging to her counter. 'They can't do this!' she cried. 'My dream! What about my dream?' She slumped to her knees. 'The biscuits! The restaurants! The Dotty Dash Show on TV!'

'Hiya!' Jack felt a tug at his sleeve, and a freckled face beamed up at him. Coco was crouching by his chair. 'So there you are!' she said. 'Been looking all over. I think the invasion's off. I've searched everywhere, and I can't find any aliens.' She looked at Jack and frowned. 'What's the matter? I thought you'd be pleased.'

'Outside,' Jack whispered. 'We need to talk.'

'What's up?' asked Coco.

'Not much.' Jack pulled her away from the tent. 'Just a small disaster.'

'Are you all right?' said Coco, peering

at the side of his face. 'Your earlobes have gone bright pink.'

'No,' Jack croaked. 'I'm not all right.' He could feel a knot in his tummy slowly twisting tighter. 'The Cake-Off's over, Coco. Finished! Ruined! Kaput!'

'What d'you mean? It's only round one.'

'The judge has gone missing, and d'you want to know why?' Jack gazed at his feet, his lower lip trembling. 'Because . . . because we shut him in a Port-a-Lav and blasted him into the stratosphere!'

'No way!' said Coco. 'You mean that grumpy old man in the field? The one with the manky hat?'

Pablo nodded. 'Huk-huk-huk!'

'Yep,' said Jack. 'That was Lord Crumble, the Cake-Off judge.'

She clapped her hand to her mouth and spluttered.

'It's not funny. It's a fiasco of fantastic proportions! They'll have to cancel the competition now, and my mum's already going berserk.'

'We'll sort it,' she said. 'It can't be that hard.'

'How? He'll be flying over the pyramids in fifteen minutes.'

'Hmm . . .' Coco twizzled a pigtail and scratched the tip of her nose. 'I know!' she said. 'I'll draw him.'

'*You?* Draw Lord Crumble? Have you dented your brainbox?'

'Why not? I'm really good at drawing old men. I did a picture of my dad for his birthday, with all the wrinkles and everything. It practically looked like a photo.'

'Hukka–hukka!' Pablo was hopping on the spot, his green pom-pom bouncing.

'See? Pablo thinks it's a great idea.' She shuffled her backpack off and pulled out her notebook. 'Hold this, will you?' In went her arm and out came Jack's feather. 'Now,' she said, 'what was Lord Crumble wearing, again?'

SEVEN

Jack staggered backwards. He looked the man up and down, from the brim of his Stetson hat to the tips of his pointed boots. *One thing's for sure,* he thought to himself. *That's definitely not Lord Crumble.*

'Howdy!' the man said, tilting his hat. 'Ma name's Crocker. Betty Crocker.'

Jack gulped. 'I'm . . . er – Jack.'

Betty nodded slowly. 'Erjack . . .' He stroked his stubbly chin. 'I ain't never heard that name before. You from these parts, boy?'

Jack looked at Coco: she was grinning from ear to ear. 'Um . . . I think there's been some sort of mistake.'

Betty patted his holsters and frowned. 'Well, shoot ma buttocks an' call me a biscuit, I'll say there's bin a mistake – some crawlin' critter's stolen ma pistols.'

Oh no!

Kelly-Ann was striding from the tent, followed by a man in black, wearing headphones.

'Ah, there you are! Kelly-Ann Caraway from Curtly Ambrose TV.' She grasped Betty's hand and flashed him a smile. 'Lord Crumble, I presume.'

'Call me Betty,' said Betty. 'I can't be doing with no fancy names. I'm just a simple cowpoke, with a raw hide to prove it.'

'And this is Quentin, our cameraman,' said Kelly-Ann.

'Whoa!' Betty took a step back. 'Easy there, Sheriff – I ain't lookin' to start no trouble here. A man don't need trouble like he don't needs a bath, an' I ain't had a bath in fifteen years.'

Kelly-Ann blinked and pressed a hanky to her nose. The cameraman scratched his head.

'Yes, siree!' Betty slapped his thigh. 'Just so long as I got a fire to cook ma beans an' a rock to rest ma head on, I'm as happy as a black-tailed jack-rabbit in a cabbage patch!'

Please, thought Jack. *Somebody make him stop!*

'Why,' said Betty, 'sometimes I get to thinkin' that all a man needs in this world is a horse to ride an' a star to guide him by ...'

'What a lovely thought,' said Kelly-Ann as she guided Betty towards the tent. 'The contestants are ready and waiting – I do hope you're hungry.'

'Yes, ma'am,' said Betty, rubbing his belly. 'I'm starvin' like a coyote who ain't seen a racoon in a week.'

Kelly-Ann pulled back the tent flap . . .

. . . and Betty sauntered into the tent – spurs clanking, leather boots squeaking, one hand hooked in his belt and the other tipping his hat to the ladies.

Jack turned to Coco. 'Tell me something,' he said. ''Cos I'm a little bit confused. I thought you were s'posed to be drawing Lord Crumble.'

Coco shrugged. 'Must've forgotten what he looked like, I s'pose.'

'Right,' said Jack. He could feel his chest heaving. 'So, you drew a cowboy called Betty instead?'

'What's the problem? He talks weird and he wears a hat. Who's gonna notice the difference?'

'You heard him!' cried Jack. 'He sleeps on a rock! He eats raccoons! He'll be riding into the High Street and robbing a bank before lunchtime!'

'Haark!' screeched Pablo, flapping his wings.

'Now look! You've scared the living daylights out of Pablo.' Jack folded his arms and glared at her. 'That's the very last time you're using my feather.'

'LADIES AND GENTLEMEN, PLEASE TAKE YOUR SEATS. THE JUDGING IS ABOUT TO COMMENCE!'

Coco pulled back the flap and peeked into the tent. 'Come on, you two – it's starting.'

The contestants were waiting at the presentation table, smoothing down their aprons and straightening their platters. The camera panned along the row of cakes: a stegosaurus with almond plates . . . a chocolate-coated triceratops . . . a dollop of dough on a platter . . . and a Tyrannosaurus rex rearing up from its plate; green mouth agape, fangs dripping red, and eyes blazing.

'That's the doctor's,' said the lady in

the hat. 'He's amazing. Ever so modest.'

Kelly-Ann tapped her microphone and flashed her teeth at the camera. 'It's my *huge* pleasure to present the first contestant in the dinosaur round. Ladies and gentlemen, please give an extra-special welcome to Dr Spleen, eight-times champion of the Curtly Ambrose Cake-Off!'

The audience burst into applause as the doctor's pale face filled the screen.

'And isn't this fabulous?' said Kelly-Ann, looking down at his Tyrannosaurus rex. 'The detail's incredible!'

Doctor Spleen smiled and tilted his head.

'Now . . .' said Kelly-Ann. 'Our very

own Cake-Off judge is going to test the sponge.' She looked around. 'Lord Crumble?'

'I don't believe it,' Jack groaned. 'What's he doing now?'

Betty was crouching on the floor, peeking over the edge of the table, frowning at the Tyrannosaurus rex. In one swift movement, he jumped to his feet, tugged off his hat and slammed it over the doctor's cake.

Kelly-Ann lurched forwards. 'Lord Crumble, *please* – would you –'

'Stand back, lady!' said Betty, barring her way with his arm. 'You don't wanna mess with this little critter – it's wilder than a snappin' turtle!' He snatched up a cake knife from the table and held it over his hat. 'One false move an' it'll bite your hand clean off an' spit out ya fingers one by one.'

And – *bam!* Betty stabbed his Stetson. Over and over. *Bam! Bam! Bam!*

Dr Spleen stiffened.

The audience gasped.

'*Extraordinary* behaviour,' said the lady in the hat.

'I knew it!' Jack squealed. 'He's a maniac, Coco – he shouldn't be allowed out in public.'

'Thank you, Lord Crumble,' said Kelly-Ann, dabbing at her forehead with her hanky. 'Time to taste the cake!'

'Huh?' said Betty. 'Ya mean this here

critter's a *cake*?' Slowly, he lifted his Stetson and peered under its brim. 'Well, who'd a-thunk it? A green cake!' He stared down at the crumbs and shook his head. 'An' there was I thinkin' it was of them swamp-beasts like the one I found last summer, underneath ma Aunt Esmerelda's porch.' He picked up a piece of sponge and popped it into his mouth. 'Mmm . . . For a green cake, it don't taste bad. Not unlike ma Aunt Esmerelda's River-Mud Pie.'

Dr Spleen narrowed his eyes.

'Yes siree!' said Betty. 'My Aunt Esmerelda – you should see her dance! Why, she takes out her teeth and she pulls up her skirts and then she starts a-jumpin' an' a-leapin'.' He cocked his hat forward and hooked his thumbs into his belt. 'Yee-haww!' he yelled, hopping and skipping, spurs flashing and heels clicking.

'What fun!' said Kelly-Ann, through gritted teeth. 'What a character your Aunt Esmerelda must be. Now –'

'Yes, sir – ma'am,' panted Betty. 'An' you should see her after a pint of whisky, why she –'

'Let's move on to contestant number two,' said Kelly-Ann. She checked her clipboard. 'A vanilla-coated pterosaur filled with pineapple jam, with a hazelnut and pistachio dusting.'

Betty gave the pterosaur a prod.

'I can't watch,' said Jack, covering his eyes with his hands.

The audience gasped again.

'Uh-oh,' said Coco. 'Betty's chucked it into the air.'

'No . . .' Jack moaned, rocking to and fro.

'Wow,' said Coco. 'That's clever. He caught it in his Stetson!'

'Haaark!' screeched Pablo.

'Duck!' someone shouted.

Jack peeked out through his fingers: the hazelnut and pistachio-dusted pterosaur was hurtling towards them. Everyone ducked as it soared over head and out through the entrance.

'And this,' said Kelly-Ann, as she scrambled to her feet, 'is contestant number three.' She patted her hair and straightened her skirt. 'Please give a very warm welcome to Mrs Dorothy Dash!'

'Huk-huk-huk!' cheered Pablo, his

little green pom-pom bouncing up and down.

Mum curtseyed. 'Lord Fumble!' she breathed. 'I do hope you like my porridge-based diplodocus.' She patted a large blue packet on the table. 'I've used only the finest ingredients.'

Uh-oh . . . thought Jack. *I've seen that packet before.*

'Premium Norwegian Oats!' said Mum.

Oh no, they're not! thought Jack. He nudged Coco and pointed at the counter. 'The packet,' he squeaked. 'Look at the packet!'

'The Penguin Poop Deodoriser Granules!' Coco giggled. 'Betty's gonna go ballistic!'

'Hmm . . .' Betty pulled the tail off the diplodocus and waggled it in the air. 'Nice 'n' slippery, like a catfish in a creek.'

'Uh-oh,' said Coco. 'It's going in.'

Mum was leaning forwards, wringing and twisting her hands.

Betty squeezed his eyes tight as he swallowed and wiped his mouth on his sleeve.

Jack pushed back his chair. 'Coco? Pablo? I think we should leave.'

'Hot diggity!' Betty slammed his fist on the table. 'Ma'am, I never tasted nothin' finer in all my doggone days! Why, I could lay down here and turn ma boots to the sun, and I'd be one mighty contented cowboy.'

'W-what's he on about?' said Jack.

'Dunno,' said Coco. 'But he liked it.'

'Your Lordship . . .?' Kelly-Ann coughed. 'If I might introduce you to our next contestant . . .'

'There's more?' said Betty, rubbing his belly. 'I ain't eaten so good since Big Nose George barbecued a bison down in Phoenix City. Makes me wanna do what a cowboy does best.' He climbed on to the kitchen counter and stood on his head. 'Feed me, ma'am – I'm ready and waitin'!'

Jack lurched to his feet, and he staggered outside.

A ripple of applause filled the air. People came spilling out of the tent, muttering and shaking their heads.

'Look,' said Coco. 'There's your mum!'

Mrs Dash was waving. She did a pirouette. 'Dumpling!' she called. 'I'm through to the semis!'

Coco clapped her hands. 'I knew it!' she cried. 'She's going to be famous.'

'Uh-oh,' said Jack. 'Here comes Betty.'

Tipping his Stetson forwards, Betty swaggered across the lawn. 'Hold it right there!' His eyes narrowed as he looked from Jack . . . to Coco . . . to Pablo. 'Which one of you no-good low-down rustlers has stolen ma horse?'

Pablo shrugged.

Coco shook her head.

'Um . . . I don't think you brought a horse with you,' said Jack.

'Is your brain made out of corn chips, mister? Everybody knows cowboys ride horses, sure as beans is beans and rattlers eat frogs.' Betty turned to scan the crowd of people gathering on the lawn. 'Why, I'm gonna find that two-bit, dirt-crawlin' culprit and show 'em a piece of my mind.'

'No!' Jack yelped, grabbing him by the arm. 'Wait here! Give me five minutes, Betty – I promise you, I'll find your horse.'

'Five minutes?' Betty smiled. 'Well, now you're talkin', Erjack!'

EIGHt

Coco scanned the car park and shook her head. 'Nope,' she said. 'I definitely can't see any horses.'

'Shh!' Jack peeked round the side of the big blue truck. He sat on the buggy-board and reached out his hand. 'Pass me my magic feather.'

She reached into her backpack. 'I hope you know what you're doing.'

'I know what I'm doing, all right,' said Jack. 'You got us into this mess, and I'm gonna get us out of it.'

He smoothed the notepad on to his knee and twirled his feather in his hand.

It shimmered like a flame. *Take it slowly,* he said to himself, as he lowered the nib to the paper. He drew a long sloping line for the nose with a wiggle at the bottom.

Pablo huffed.

Coco giggled. 'What's *that*?'

'They're the lips, of course.'

'They're a bit big, aren't they?' said Coco. 'It's starting to look like a goldfish. Tell you what, why don't you let –'

'Keep your freckled face out of this, will you? You've caused enough trouble as it is.' Jack drew two little circles, side by side. 'Those are the nostrils and these are the ears . . .' And he added a pair of triangles. He drew an arc for the neck, then a . . . **scribble-scribble-scribble**. '

And this . . .' he said.

'Don't tell me,' said Coco. 'It's a toothbrush.'

'Haaark!' Pablo toppled over and rolled around on the grass.

Jack sighed. 'It's the mane, of course. Will you two stop interrupting? I'm actually finding it hard to concentrate, and now the body's gone weird.'

Coco leaned over his shoulder and frowned. 'The whole thing looks weird if you ask me.'

'I'm not asking you, OK?' Jack took a deep breath. He sketched four long legs and a tail and he added a saddle and a pair of reins. He placed the notepad on the ground and scrambled to his feet. 'Stand back,' he said. 'She might get frisky.'

Coco stared at the notepad.

Pablo cocked his head.

Jack closed his eyes, he crossed his fingers and –

ZAP!

'Wow!' said Coco.

'Haark!' squawked Pablo.

'Yes!' cried Jack, pumping his fist in the air. She was magnificent: broad of shoulder, long of mane, and covered in auburn fur. She gazed at Jack from under her eyelashes, chewing slowly.

'Are you *sure* that's a horse?' said Coco.

''Course I'm sure! Look how big and strong she is – I think she must be a thoroughbred.'

'Right.' Coco pointed at the ground. 'Is that why she's got weird paws?'

Huh? Jack looked at the animal's feet: they were divided down the middle like two fat toes. 'Um . . . she's probably a Kentucky Split-Hoofed Mustang. There's loads of mud in Kentucky. Stops them from sliding about.'

Coco peered a little closer. 'Her knees are very knobbly.'

'It's all that running and jumping,' said Jack. 'Builds up their leg muscles.'

'*OK* . . .' Coco stood on her tiptoes and pointed. 'So what's with the massive lump?'

'What?' Jack blinked. On the creature's back was a large, rounded hump, tufted with orange hair.

'D'you know something, Jack? I think it's a camel.'

No way, he thought. *I drew a horse! I know I did.*

The animal turned her gaze on Pablo. She curled back her upper lip: foam was collecting round her yellow teeth.

'Uh-oh,' said Coco. 'I think she's gonna –'

'**Phssssssssssssttttt!**' A flobbit of spittle arced through the air and – *splat!* – it landed on Pablo's tummy.

'Haark!' screeched Pablo and tumbled backwards.

Coco folded her arms. 'See?' she said. 'Definitely a camel.'

'Nooo!' Jack wailed. 'She can't be!' But, deep in the soles of his trainers, he knew she was right. He gazed at the heavens and swallowed.

'Guess what?' said Coco, poking her head around the side of the truck. 'Betty's coming over.'

'Quick! Quick! We need to find somewhere to hide!' Jack tried the door handle on the van. He rattled and squeezed – it was locked! He fell to his knees and peered underneath.

'Well, sizzlin' scorpions and refried beans! How ya doin', Trigger?' Betty patted the camel's neck. 'An' there was I thinkin' these yellow-bellied bandits had been and gone and sold you at the county fair.'

The camel nibbled at a clump of grass.

Betty grabbed a tuft of fur in his fists and swung his leg up as high as it would go. Grunting and panting, he tried to heave himself up. Down he slid again, landing on the grass with a *thud!*

The camel raised her head. She eyed Betty from under her lashes, chewing sideways.

'My, my, my!' Betty rubbed his chin. 'What they been feeding you, Trigger? 'Cos you sure have grown a whole bunch.' He took eight steps back and tilted his Stetson. 'One . . . two . . . three . . .' He ran – he jumped – he flew through the air. Flinging his arms around her neck, he hauled himself on to her hump. 'Yes siree!' Betty tipped his hat back and straightened his neckerchief. 'Sure is good to be back in the saddle.'

'I think you better get down now,' said Jack. 'Round two's about to start.'

'Ma belly's full and ma horse is rested. It's time to hit the trail.'

'But . . . but you can't leave now.'

'Ain't no time like the present.' Betty raised his face to the sky. 'The sun's high an' the wind's in from the south. It's time to find some place that a man can call his home.' He gathered up his reins and sighed. 'I ain't found it yet, and some days it feels like I never will. But a man's gotta keep on searchin', elsewise he'll never rest happy.' He clicked his tongue. 'Ya ready, Trigger?'

The camel snorted.

Betty dug his heels into her bulging sides. With a flick of her tail, she lolloped across the lawn, with Betty clinging on to her hump, joggling up and down.

NINE

'Betty's gone AWOL,' said Jack. 'What are we going to do?'

'Uh-oh,' said Coco. 'It's Kelly-Ann!'

The presenter was striding from the tent. 'Well?' She planted her hands on her hips and turned to Quentin, the cameraman. 'Where's His Lordship gone now?'

Quentin grimaced and shook his head.

'People warned me,' said Kelly-Ann. 'They said he's "a bit peculiar". "Quite a character", they said. But I wasn't prepared for this! All that talk about saddles and jackrabbits? Performing a cartwheel in the baking arena? The man's unhinged! And now he's gone heaven-knows-where – all by himself – in no fit state! He's probably in a hedge somewhere, talking to twigs.'

Quentin studied his fingernails.

'I give up!' said Kelly-Ann. 'We'll just have to start without him. If he's not back for the judging at four o'clock, I'm going to report him missing.'

She spun on her high heels and strode back into the tent.

'*LADIES AND GENTLEMEN, PLEASE TAKE YOUR SEATS. THE FINAL ROUND IS ABOUT TO COMMENCE!*'

'What's up?' whispered Coco. 'You're making a funny noise.'

'You heard her,' Jack replied. 'She's going to report Betty missing. And you know what that means, don't you?'

'They'll cancel the Cake-Off and your mum'll have a meltdown?'

'It's worse than that,' said Jack. 'They'll send out a search party! Sniffer dogs, helicopters – the lot! They'll look in the fields and gather incriminating evidence. It's probably all on CCTV. The trombone! The yaks! The Port-a-Lav! They'll . . . they'll find out what we did!' He buried his head in his hands. 'Oh, we're in trouble right up to our nostrils.'

'Not if we find Betty first.'

'And how are we going to do that?' he wailed. 'He's hit the trail. He could be anywhere by now, and the judging starts in an hour!'

Coco tugged at the rope, the sail swung round and – *rattle-bump-bump* – they swerved off the lawn and on to the drive.

'It's hopeless,' said Jack, wiping his forehead. 'We've been through the woods seven times already and now we're back where we started. We've got thirty minutes tops, Coco – we're running out of time.'

'We never checked the castle,' she said.

'The . . . the castle?' Jack looked up at its cold grey walls, with its arches and towers and its little slitted windows. 'But it's private property. They *definitely* won't be in there.'

Coco shrugged. 'It's worth a try.'

She pulled the rope, the sail billowed and they took off up the drive.

Here we go again, thought Jack. 'Slow down, will you?' he called. 'My Achilles tendon's about to snap!'

'Can't hear you,' she yelled as they clattered over the drawbridge.

'Harrk!' screeched Pablo, his orange knees knocking.

'Coco?' Jack clutched the mast and looked over the side at the murky depths of the moat. 'This is a bad idea!'

'Wahoo!' she hollered as they thundered through a huge stone arch, clattered over a cobbled courtyard and cruised through a doorway into the Great Hall. She wrenched at the rope, the sail swung round and they slammed to a halt by the staircase.

Jack stumbled off the buggy-board and rubbed his shoulder. 'I – I think I've dislodged my vertebra.' He peered through the gloom at the worn stone steps, which led up to a long, narrow balcony overlooking the hall. He squinted at a tattered red flag hanging from its rail, and up, up, up at the ancient beams, soaring high above his head.

'Isn't this amazing?' said Coco. 'An

actual real castle! Bet you anything it's haunted.'

Jack wound his scarf tight around his neck and shivered. 'Don't be daft. Everybody knows that ghosts are extinct. Anyway,' he said, tugging at her arm, 'looks like Betty and Trigger aren't in here. I really think we should —'

'Over there!' She was pointing towards a suit of armour, which stood in the corner, nearly two metres tall. She scampered across the hall, rose on to her tiptoes and — *clunck!* — flipped up the visor. 'Yoo-hoo! Anybody home?'

'Thought so,' said Jack, heading back towards the entrance. 'There's nobody here. Let's go and . . . Coco?' He could hear the squeak of her trainers as she disappeared into the shadows. He checked over his shoulders, right then left. He peeked behind a pillar. 'C-Coco?' His voice bounced around the walls. 'W-where are you?'

'Up here, you dumb-bum!'

She was high above him on the balcony now. He could see her silhouette: a pair of pigtails, a hand waving.

'What are you doing up there, you fruitcake?'

'Looking for Betty and Trigger, of course.'

Jack sighed. He climbed up the steps, one by one. He glanced round the balcony and folded his arms. 'Surprise, surprise! They're not up here.'

'Look!' At the far end was a door, its brass knob shining in the dark. 'D'you reckon they've gone through there?'

'When will you get it into your fruit-filled brain? The castle's empty. There's nobody here. And if we don't find –'

'Shh!' She lifted a pigtail and leaned over the balcony rail. 'Did you hear that?'

Plip-plap . . . plip-plap . . .

Uh-oh, thought Jack. *I can hear it all right.*

'Down there,' she whispered. 'Something's moving but I can't see what it is.'

Plip-plap . . . plip-plap . . .

Jack felt his mouth go dry. *It's getting louder.* He stepped away from the balcony rail, flattening his back against the wall. *It's coming up the stairs!*

Plip-plap . . . plip-plap . . .

'Oooh!' squealed Coco. 'It's Pablo!'

'Huk-huk-huk!'

Gone were the paper bag, the rubber gloves and the plastic flowerpot with the pom-pom glued to the top. There was pondweed on his head and tangled in his tail, his feathers were stuck together in spikes and his tummy was stained emerald green.

'Pooey,' said Coco. 'He smells worse than my gran's fridge.'

'He must've fallen into the moat.' Jack fell to his knees and grasped Pablo's slimy wing. 'Are you OK?'

Pablo squeezed his eyes shut. He opened his beak and – 'Huk-huk-heurggh!' A tadpole plopped on to the floor.

Jack turned to Coco. 'Now see what you've done? I told you we were driving that buggy too fast.'

'He's a penguin, you Dilbert. I think he knows how to swim.'

'Did you see the colour of that water? It must be full of all sorts – he's probably swallowed a poisonous bacterium.'

'Jack?' hissed Coco. 'There's something behind him!'

On the staircase, halfway down, blazed a pair of yellow eyes.

'Hnnnnfff!' Pablo was trembling all over now.

'Are you *sure* ghosts are extinct?' whispered Coco. ''Cos that looks like one to me.'

Jack seized her by the arm. 'It's c-coming c-closer!' he croaked.

Slowly, silently, the yellow eyes advanced up the steps. A talon emerged into the light, reaching forwards, and a long, high shriek pierced the darkness: '**OOAOWAAAARGHH**!'

Jack clutched at his heart. He felt his blood curdle.

'Aww,' said Coco. 'It's a peahen.'

'You — you *what*?'

'You know,' she said. 'One of those lady peacocks.'

'Pheeeet!' The peahen stepped on to

the balcony, the spray of blue feathers on top of her head shimmering in the half-light. She craned her neck and rubbed her cheek against Pablo's wing.

'Hssst!' hissed Pablo, backing away.

'Isn't that adorable?' said Coco. 'She wants to be friends. Let's call her Margot. What d'you think?'

'Margot! Beryl! Mildred! Call her anything you like. We've gotta get out of here, now!'

'You must be joking. The fun's only just started. Come on!' she called, as she scuttled off down the balcony.

'Wait! Stop! What are you doing?'

Coco twisted the doorknob and disappeared inside.

tEN

'Coco? Are you in there?'

Jack stepped through the door and blinked: sunlight fell from an arched window across a dusty table, which stretched the length of the room. In the centre sat a bowl of withered apples and a mouldy bunch of grapes. At the far end, a single place was set, with a knife and a fork and a plate.

Where is she? thought Jack. *Where's The Fruitcake gone now?*

He walked along the row of portraits, which were hanging on the wall, each with a plaque underneath: *Lord Ethelred*

Crumble . . . Lord Algernon Crumble . . . Lord Horatio Crumble III . . .

Plip-plap, plip-plap – he could hear Pablo behind him, and the *scrabble-scrabble-scrabble* of Margot's claws on the flagstones.

Lord Oswald Crumble . . . Lord Cuthbert Crumble . . . Lord Percy Tankred Witherspoon Crumble . . .

That's him – Lord Percy Tankred Witherspoon Crumble! Jack looked up at the wrinkled face and a pair of pale blue eyes gazed back at him. *He'll be flying over the Indian Ocean by now. He's probably sitting on the toilet seat, hammering at the door.* Jack swallowed. He looked at Lord Crumble's weary mouth, which was sagging at the corners. A mouth that hadn't smiled for years and years and years.

'Jack?'

He spun around. 'Coco? Where've you been?'

She pointed to a door at the end of the room, and grinned. 'Guess what,' she said. 'I've found them!'

Betty's eyes were closed and his mouth was open. He lay, snoring, in a sheet, which was slung like a hammock from the four-poster bed. Beside him stood Trigger, her head inside a wardrobe, chewing at the cord of a silk dressing-gown.

'What are they doing in here?' Jack squeaked. 'This is Lord Crumble's bedroom.'

Tick, tock. Tick, tock. The hands on the bedside clock were pointing at ten to four.

'Betty?' Jack shook him by the shoulder. 'You gotta wake up. You're s'posed to be judging round two.'

'Huk!' squawked Pablo.

'Pheeeet!' chirped Margot.

'Hmmph!' snorted Betty, and rolled on to his side.

'Leave this to me.' Coco jabbed Betty's chest with her forefinger and yelled in to his ear. 'Oi! Shift it, dozy-knickers!'

Betty lurched upright. The hammock flipped over and flung him on to the floor.

'Don't nobody move!' He leaped to his feet, snatched up a hairbrush from the bedside table and pointed it at Jack. 'OK, mister, put ya hands up!'

Jack threw his arms in the air.

'Now, be a good cowboy,' said Coco, 'and put the hairbrush down.'

Betty narrowed his eyes. He turned the brush on Coco, his fingers tightening round the handle, his knuckles turning white.

No-no-no, thought Jack. *This is all going monstrously wrong.* 'Coco,' he squawked. 'For the love of cheese toasties, do what he says!'

Coco picked up Betty's hat from the floor and slapped it on his head. 'We're leaving.'

'Well, now,' said Betty. 'Didn't figure it was you. My eyes ain't seein' straight. Like that time in Sacramento when me an' Big Nose George went –'

'Listen,' said Coco. 'If you're not back in ten minutes, Kelly-Ann's gonna report you missing.'

'Huh?'

Trigger flicked her tail, still chewing slowly.

'She's gonna tell the sheriff,' said Coco.

'The sheriff?' said Betty. 'Sweet Jiminy – you shoulda said!'

Trigger peered over the balcony to the Great Hall below, with Betty perched high on her hump.

'Atta girl!' said Betty. 'You can do it.'

Trigger snorted. She shook her head.

'C'mon!' said Betty, kick-kick-kicking his heels into her bulging sides. 'Ain't much more than a gentle slope.'

Trigger curled back her lip, foam gathering round her muzzle.

'S'no good,' said Jack. 'You'll have to leave her here.'

Betty shook his head. 'No ways. Trigger stays, I stays.'

'Five minutes!' Jack cried. 'We've got five minutes!'

'**OOAOWAAAARGHH**!' shrieked Margot, flapping her wings.

Trigger's eyes widened. Her nostrils flared. Betty lurched backwards as she reared up on to her hind feet and – *clatter-bang-whoosh* – she launched herself downstairs.

'Yee-haww!' yelled Betty, clutching the camel's hump with one hand and waving his hat with the other. 'Go, Trigger, you ol' buckin' mustang!'

Bang! Bang! Bang! She careered down the steps, legs splayed and tail swinging.

'Watch out!' cried Jack. 'The buggy!'

Trigger skidded off the bottom step and on to the buggy-board, with Betty still clinging to her hump. Off they sailed, through the Great Hall and out of the door. Jack could hear the clatter of wheels as they crossed the courtyard and rattled over the drawbridge.

ELEVEN

The sail buggy was lying outside the Cake-Off tent, its mast broken, the board in splinters and the axle twisted skyward. Trigger was chewing its sail.

'Where's Betty?' said Jack.

'I think he went inside,' said Coco, pointing to a tear in the side of the tent.

Jack poked his head through the rip and gasped: a small crowd had gathered around a woman who was sprawled on the ground. A man was kneeling beside her, fanning her face with a hat.

'Coco?' he croaked. 'There's been an accident.'

'Ooh!' she squealed. 'Let's have a look!' She scooched up beside him and thrust her head through the hole. 'It's that lady from the audience. And there's Betty – under the presentation table!'

Gripping on to the table leg, Betty crawled out and hauled himself to his feet. 'Hooo!' He shook his head, slapped the side of his face and adjusted his Stetson. 'I reckons I was flying faster than a bluebird with a buzzard on its tail. An' if it weren't for that there lady standin' in my way, why – I'd be in South Dakota by now!'

'LADIES AND GENTLEMEN, THE JUDGING OF THE SEMI-FINALS IS ABOUT TO COMMENCE.'

One by one, the contestants were

bringing their cakes to the table. Kelly-Ann beamed at the camera.

'Yummy!' Coco nudged Jack in the ribs and pointed across the tent. 'Look at that ginormous chocolate one with the pink marshmallows on top.'

Jack heard a snort. He turned around. 'Uh-oh,' he said. 'I think Trigger heard you.'

The camel was ambling across the lawn towards them, her nostrils quivering.

'Oh no, you don't!' Jack grabbed her by the reins and pulled her away. 'You're not going in there, you great greedy, humped-back flubber-mouth.'

Trigger gazed down at him. She curled her lip back and clamped her teeth around his scarf. She closed her eyes and began to chew it.

'Coco?' he wheezed. 'Help me out here, will you?'

'Not now,' she called over her shoulder. 'It's getting exciting. Betty's got a lasso.'

'Coco, *please*!' Jack rasped, tugging at his scarf. 'I'm actually finding it hard to breathe.'

'Wahey!' She turned to him and beamed. 'He's caught it, Jack! Betty's lassoed the chocolate cake!' Her head disappeared through the hole again. 'This is amazing – he's swinging it round his head.'

Jack clawed at his throat with one hand and pulled at his scarf with the other.

He sank to his knees, gulping and panting for air.

'I can see your mum,' said Coco. 'She's taking her cake out of the oven. There's smoke everywhere! I think she's burned it.'

'My scarf!' gasped Jack. 'Trigger's taken my scarf!'

The camel was wandering towards the car park now, with her tail swinging and a strand of blue wool trailing behind her.

'Hukka-hukka-hukka!' And here came Pablo, scuttling over the grass.

Jack scrambled to his feet. 'What is it?' he said. 'What's the matter?'

Pablo pointed his wing at Margot, who was strutting towards them, across the lawn.

'You're not gonna believe it!' said Coco. 'Betty just karate chopped your mum's cake in half.'

'**OOAOWAAAARGHH**!' shrieked Margot.

'Haaaaaaark!' squawked Pablo, hiding behind Jack's leg.

'Will you lot be quiet? Betty's judging.' Coco looked back through the hole. 'He's taking a bite. He's trying to swallow. He's smiling, Jack – I think he liked it! *Yes!*' she cried, and punched the air. 'Your mum's through to the final!'

The audience was leaving the tent, chatting in twos and threes; the crew with microphones and headsets emerged, and here came Kelly-Ann with her clipboard, followed by Quentin the cameraman.

'Oh, I can't wait for tomorrow!' Coco scooped up Pablo and bundled him into her backpack. 'Just think – if your mum wins she'll start wearing sunglasses and riding around town in a stretch limo.'

'It won't be easy,' said Jack. 'She's gotta beat Dr Spleen first.'

'Look!' said Coco. 'He's over there. Why's he staring at Margot like that?'

Dr Spleen was crouched on the grass, his stethoscope dangling from his neck and holding his big black bag. He reached out a bony hand to pat the peahen's head.

'Well, howdy there, doc!' Betty swaggered out and slapped him on the back. 'This here Cake-Off sure is hottin' up – I figures ya gonna need more luck tomorrow than a speckled hen in a snake pit!' He tipped his hat to Jack. 'See ya at sun up, Erjack. Me and Trigger are gonna find us a clearin', cook up some beans and stare at the stars till our eyes grow heavy.'

'Pheet!' Margot scuttled after Betty as he strode towards the car park.

Dr Spleen smiled to himself, rubbing his hands as he watched her go.

tWELVE

Yeuurch! Jack twitched his nose. What was that smell? Rotten spinach? Boiled vests? *I've smelt it before – I know I have.* He rubbed his eyes. *Pondweed . . .* he thought. *Definitely pondweed.*

'Huk!' Pablo tugged at the duvet.

'You stink,' said Jack. 'Go away.'

'Huk-huk!' He was jabbing at Jack's elbow with his beak.

'Ouch!' Jack pulled his pillow over his head. 'It's the middle of the night, I've had a hard day and I'm trying to sleep.'

'HAAAAARK!' screeched the penguin. Jack could hear him scuffling across the floor and *tap-tappity-tap* – at his bedroom door.

'OK, OK! I'm coming.' Jack slid out of bed, pulled the door open and stumbled on to the landing: Pablo was standing in a patch of moonlight, pointing his beak at the back window that looked on to the garden.

'Hukka–hukka–hukka!'

'Keep your beak shut, will you? You'll wake up Mum and Dad.' Jack squished his nose to the glass. What was going on down there? An orange glow . . . shadows moving . . . Slowly, carefully, he eased the window open. 'That's weird,' he whispered, twitching his nose. 'It smells like a bonfire.' He poked his head outside.

'Great hairy grasshoppers – it *is* a bonfire!'

'**OOAOWAAAARGHH**!'

Jack felt the windowpane rattle and the hairs on his arms stand on end.

'Yoo-hoo!' A head with a pair of pigtails popped out of a window next door. 'Did you hear that?' she called. 'It's Margot. Bet you anything she's looking for Pablo.'

Pablo froze, his feathers bristling.

'I don't get it,' said Jack. 'How did she even find us?'

'Probably wasn't that hard,' said Coco. 'You can smell him from half a mile away. Ooh look – Trigger's down there too!'

''Course it's not Trigger. She's at the castle. It must be a badger or something.'

'Wowza,' said Coco. 'That's one big badger.'

Jack squinted through the darkness: over by the hedge he could see a shape. Four skinny legs and a hump. Even in the flickering firelight, it was unmistakable. He heard the snap of a twig and then the rustle of leaves.

Coco giggled. 'There goes the apple tree.'

'*What?*' he cried. 'My Dad'll freak! He'll flip his widget. He'll –'

'Shh!' Coco was cupping her hand to her ear. 'D'you hear that? Someone's singing.'

Jack could hear *something* all right, but it didn't sound much like singing – more

like the squeal of broken brakes on a very
rusty bike.

'*My lonesome heart aches for home . . .*'

Jack curled up his toes and gritted his
teeth.

'It's Betty,' said Coco. 'Over by the
lettuces.' She giggled again. 'He's set up
camp in your garden.'

'No matter where I roam . . .' sang Betty.

Jack felt his heart plummet. 'How?' he croaked. 'How did they get in?'

'Through the hedge, of course,' said Coco. 'See? They've made a massive hole.'

'A hole?' Jack wailed. 'In my dad's hedge? W–what's he gonna say?'

And then the screeching started again.

'**OOAOWAAAARGHH**!'

'Aww,' said Coco. 'Margot's joining in!'

Pablo shivered all over. He buried his head under his wing.

'I do not know . . .' sang Betty, 'where should I go . . .'

'**OOAOWAAAARGHH**!' shrieked Margot.

And off scuttled Pablo, back to Jack's bedroom.

'Uh-oh,' said Coco. 'That's *my* dad.'

A light went on in Coco's house. A scrape . . . a clunk . . . and the window beneath her opened: a pair of hairy hands was holding a plastic bucket. Jack backed away, his heart thumping.

He heard a *SPLASH!* and then a clatter as the bucket hit the ground.

The garden went dark.

There was silence in Quarantine Street.

tHIRtEEN

'I had a dream.' Mrs Dash put down her teacup and shivered. 'It was magical — there was beautiful music in our garden!'

Mr Dash grunted from behind his newspaper.

Uh-oh. Through the kitchen window, right behind his mum, Jack could see Betty sleeping in the boughs of the apple tree.

'Oh, Lionel.' Mum reached across the table and squeezed Dad's shoulder. 'You were singing. I never knew you could be so romantic!'

'Not me, I'm afraid.' Dad folded up

his paper and frowned. 'I hope it wasn't a trespasser trying to steal my vegetables.'

'Trespasser?' Mum's eyes widened. 'In our garden? Goodness me, how distressing!'

Please, thought Jack, as Trigger padded past the window with a lettuce in her mouth. *Don't turn around.*

'You can't be too sure these days,' said Dad. 'I'd better review the security arrangements, straight after breakfast.'

'What a good idea!' said Mum. 'We can't have trespassers in the house – just think of those muddy footprints all over my nice clean floor!' She was looking round the kitchen now. 'Where's Pablo?'

Upstairs, thought Jack. *Hiding from Margot.*

Mum was wringing her hands. 'You . . . you don't think the trespassers have kidnapped him, do you?'

'Um . . . He's having a lie-in,' said Jack. 'He's – er – feeling a bit tired.'

'Oh dear, I hope he hasn't got influenza. Mrs Tangent from down the road was in bed for a week. She's still got a runny nose.'

Tap-tap-tap.

Mum sat up, her lower lip trembling. 'What was that?'

A brown face with a spray of blue feathers was at the kitchen window. *Tappity-tap-tap-tap.* It was pecking at the glass.

Not now, Margot – please.

She   threw   back   her   head:

'**OOAOWAAAARGHH**!'

'Goodness gracious!' said Mum.

'Aha!' Dad pushed back his chair. 'I know that sound. It's a blocked pipe. There's an airlock somewhere in the plumbing.' He stood and rolled up his sleeves. 'Leave this to me, Dotty – I'll get my plunger.' And he disappeared into the hall.

Mum checked her watch and jumped to her feet. 'Is that the time? The final starts at eleven!'

I gotta get Betty out of here, thought Jack.

Mum flung the kitchen cupboard open. 'Flour . . . sugar . . . baking powder . . .' She bundled them into a box. 'I need that special ingredient. I've got to wow the judge.' She grabbed a jar from the shelf. 'Peanut butter! Yes! I'll make a peanut-butter fairy princess sitting in a jelly carriage. Must keep moving. So much to do! Measurements . . . timings . . . tiara . . . I hope I haven't forgotten anything.'

Cock-a-doodle doo!

'That'll be Dr Spleen!' said Mum. 'He's giving me a lift to the Cake-Off. Isn't that thoughtful? Such a nice man!' And she gathered her box into her arms and bustled into the hall.

Jack scuttled to the garden door and opened it a crack. 'What do you think you're playing at?' he hissed. 'I told you to go away!'

'Pheet!' Margot looked up at him and cocked her head to one side.

'I mean it!' Jack glanced over his shoulder – the front door was still open. He could see Mum on the pavement, loading up Doctor Spleen's car.

Great! he thought. *And here comes The Fruitcake.*

'Morning!' called Coco. 'What's Dr Purple-Lips doing outside?'

'He's driving my mum to the Cake-Off,' Jack whispered. 'Except there isn't gonna be a Cake-Off any more, cos the judge is still in the garden.'

Coco flung the back door open wide.

'Wow,' she said. 'Looks like it was hit by a tornado.'

Jack felt his knees go weak. It was even worse than he'd thought.

Where once there grew a perfect lawn, with emerald-green stripes, there was now a square of mud; where once bloomed delphiniums, veronica and peonies, a

bed of broken stalks. The lettuces had been flattened, the carrots uprooted and the courgettes squashed. The bark of the apple tree was hanging in ribbons . . . and there lay Betty in its branches, his Stetson tipped over his face.

'So what are you gonna tell to your dad?' said Coco. 'A giant badger did it?'

Jack let out a moan.

'OK,' she said, shuffling off her backpack. 'I've had a brilliant idea.' She thrust in her hand and pulled out his feather. 'I'll draw your dad a zip wire. That should cheer him up. We'll run it from the bathroom window down to the back hedge.'

'Not now, Coco – my head hurts.'

'Come on, Jack – he'll love it! I'll even draw an alligator pit underneath just to make it more exciting.'

'Give me that!' said Jack, snatching the feather from her hand. 'Why don't you try using your brain for once, or are you saving it up for a special occasion?'

'Oh well, please yourself. But don't

blame me when your dad throws a wobbly.'

The feather fizzed. It crackled and sparkled. Jack caught his breath as he turned it in his fingers. He looked out across the garden and a slow smile spread across his face.

Jack drew a rectangle for a flowerbed, which he covered in swirls and blobs. He sketched a lettuce with a squiggle – and another, and another. He made a looping line of runner beans and a great big circle for a pumpkin. *Tick, tick, tick, tick* – he drew a brand-new lawn.

'Not bad, eh? I reckon my dad'll be chuffed to pieces.' Jack tore out the page and placed it on the ground. *Any second now . . .*

'Ooh, look!' squealed Coco. 'I think there's a daisy where the rose bush used to be.'

'A daisy? Is that all?'

She pointed to the small green stalks, which were poking through the mud. 'And there's a couple of weeds over there.' She frowned and looked at Jack's feather. 'You don't think it's running out of juice, do you?'

'It's a magic feather, Coco – it doesn't run on juice. It just needs a bit more time, that's all.'

'Right.' She twizzled her pigtail. 'What time does the Cake-Off start again?'

'Eleven o'clock. We need to get moving.'

She looked at Jack and giggled. 'I can't wait for Lord Crumble to meet Betty.'

Jack swallowed. 'W-what d'you mean?'

'Well . . . if the Port-a-Lav lands outside the grocer's at 10.17, like you said, then he'll be back at the castle in time for the final. Just think!' she said. 'There'll be two Lord Crumbles!'

Jack stared at Coco. He felt his tummy lurch. 'This is a catastrophe – we've got to stop him!'

'I know,' she said. 'He's gonna be furious! Especially when he finds out Trigger ate his dressing gown. We'd better go down to the High Street straight away and wait for him to land.' She patted her backpack and winked. 'Don't worry, I've got a lollipop in here.'

'A *lollipop*?' said Jack. 'You want to meet Lord Crumble off the Port-a-Lav and give him a *lollipop*? Are you actually being serious, or did your brain fall out of your nostril?'

'We'll use it to jam the lock, you dim-bat. If it worked on my granny, it'll work on Lord Crumble.'

Jack closed his eyes and breathed a shuddering sigh. 'Come on, Betty!' he called. 'There's been a change of plan.'

'Huh?' The apple tree rustled. Betty tilted back his hat. 'That you, Erjack?'

'Move it!' yelled Coco. 'We're leaving!'

'Quit your yappin',' said Betty, replacing his Stetson. 'Ma bed's soft, ma horse is fed and I reckons this here clearing's a mighty fine place for a lie-in.'

Jack felt a stab of panic in his chest. '*Please*,' he wailed. 'We've got to go!'

'I get it,' said Betty, lowering himself to the ground. 'A cowboy knows when he ain't welcome.' He hung his head and kicked at the earth with his pointed toe. 'Ya hear that, Trigger? We're hittin' the trail again. No point stayin' where we ain't wanted.'

'OK, Coco – wait there,' said Jack, pointing to the bottom of the stairs. 'If you hear my dad, just shout.' He ran to the back door. 'Betty!' he called. 'Bring her through, and make it snappy.'

Trigger padded across the garden towards him, with Betty perched high on her hump. She stopped when she reached the doorway, and poked her nose into the hall.

'We got ourselves a problem,' said Betty. 'This door ain't big enough for the both of us.'

'You'll have to get off,' said Jack, 'and lead her through by the reins.'

'No can do,' said Betty.

Jack glanced over his shoulder. '*Please*,'

he said. 'There's no other way.'

'Now see here, mister – ya callin' me a quitter? Cowboys don't quit same as skunks don't whistle and hogs don't play the ukulele.'

'Right,' said Jack. 'Maybe you should try bending forwards.'

'Smart thinkin', Erjack.' Betty tucked in his chin and hunched himself over. He clicked his tongue. Trigger shuffled forwards a centimetre or two and then she came to a halt. 'Well, son of a gun!' came a muffled cry, from underneath Betty's Stetson. 'I do believes I'm stuck.'

'Come on – come on – *come on*!' Jack grabbed Trigger's reins and pulled. 'Shift it, will you? This is an emergency!'

'Just hold on there,' said Betty, his head wedged under the doorframe now and his hat jammed over his nose. 'It's hotter than a buffalo's armpit in here and it's gettin' kinda stuffy.'

'Don't you get it? We've got to *leave*!'

'Shh!' said Coco. She stood on her tiptoes and peered up the staircase. 'Did you hear that?' Her eyes widened. She lifted a pigtail and tilted her head. 'I think your dad's coming down.'

Jack closed his eyes. *What's he gonna say when he finds a camel in the house?* He took a deep breath. *Keep calm, Jack – think, think, think!* 'I've got it.' He turned to Betty. 'You'll just have to back out again. You can leave through the hole in the hedge, and we'll meet you in Vaccine Lane.'

Betty kicked his heels. He flicked the reins. 'Nope,' he said. 'She ain't budgin'. This horse don't work in reverse.'

Clomp-clomp-clomp – Jack could hear his father's footsteps. *He's coming – he's coming – he's coming!* He pulled and he panted and heaved. 'Shift it, you hairy-humped horror!'

FOURTEEN

'Don't worry,' said Coco. 'I'll keep your dad talking while you sort out Betty and Trigger.'

'Wait!' Jack cried. 'How am I s'posed to –'

Thump-thump-thump – she was already sprinting up the stairs.

'Hello, Coco. Are you looking for Jack?' he heard his father ask.

He sounds close, thought Jack. *Very close. I think he's on the landing.*

'Hello, Mr D,' said Coco. 'Fancy meeting you here! What a lovely morning! That's a nice pair of socks you're wearing.

Were they a birthday present?'

'Er . . . would you mind just moving out of my way?' said Dad. 'I'm trying to get downstairs.'

Coco, please, thought Jack. *Stop him!*

He heard a bang and then a giggle. 'Whoopsie!' said Coco. 'There goes my backpack.'

A ball of string, a chocolate bar, a toilet brush and an empty yoghurt pot came tumbling down the stairs.

'OOAOWAAAARGHH!'

Margot's up there too? Jack rubbed his ear and shook his head. *No. She can't be. I must be hearing things.*

'That's strange,' his dad was saying. 'I thought the blockage was in the kitchen, but I think it's coming from upstairs.'

'Yep,' said Coco. 'Sounds like a blockage in your bathroom, all right. It happened to us last Tuesday. My dad kept on hearing funny noises and – *boom!* The toilet blew right off the wall. Too much gas, apparently.'

'Gracious!' said Dad. 'Off the wall? I'd better inspect the U-bend.'

Thump-thump-thump – down came Coco. She grinned and gave Jack a thumbs-up.

'What did you tell him that for?' said Jack. 'He's gonna freak when he finds Margot in the bathroom.'

'She isn't in there, you dumb-plop. I dunno where she is.'

'Quit ya jawin' and get me outta here,' said Betty. 'Ma head's as sore as a bullfrog in a briar patch.'

Coco fished out a packet of crisps from her backpack. She ripped it open and shook it under Trigger's nose. 'Chicken and Marmite – should do the trick.'

Trigger snorted. Her eyes lit up.

Coco rattled the packet again.

Trigger craned her neck, her lower lip flapping. She shifted and she squirmed and – yes! – she stumbled into the hall.

'Whoa!' cried Betty, as he tumbled backwards on to the floor. He scrambled to his feet. 'Erjack . . .? You still there?' Grasping his Stetson by the brim, he yanked it off his face. 'Hallelujah!' he cried. 'Thank the sweet sufferin' stars, I can see!'

'Hey!' said Jack. 'Come back!'

'Mighty fine saloon you got here,' said Betty, swaggering into the kitchen. He bent down and opened the dishwasher.

'This where you keep your whisky?'

Jack heard a snort. He spun around. Trigger was poking her head around the kitchen door. 'Coco!' he cried. 'Stop her!'

Coco made a swipe for the reins. Too late! **Clip-clop-clip-clop** – Trigger was sauntering across the floor tiles.

Clang!

'Uh-oh,' said Coco. 'There goes the kettle.'

Bang!

'And that's the toaster.'

'No!' cried Jack. 'My mum's lucky tea towel!'

And into her mouth it went. **Clip-clop-clip** – Trigger paused by the sink, chewing slowly. She licked a cereal bowl with her huge pink tongue. She sniffed at a plate on the draining board and nudged it to the floor.

Crash!

'Jack?' Coco was tapping at his shoulder. 'I think that's your –'

'Dumpling?'

Hot, holy chilli peppers – Mum's in the hall!

'Oh dear, oh dear,' she was saying. 'Where *did* I put it?'

Jack clung to the kitchen table and looked at the broken chair, the fragments of china all over the floor, Betty swigging from a ketchup bottle, and Trigger with her head in the fridge, licking a packet of butter. He let out a long, low whimper.

'S'OK,' said Coco. 'Leave this to me.' She sprinted out of the kitchen and slammed the door behind her.

Jack could hear her yabbering in the hall. 'Don't worry, Mrs D – you wait here and I'll bring it out.' And back into the kitchen she skidded. 'Hurry, Jack! Your mum's forgotten her Kwik-set Jelly!'

'Right,' said Jack. 'Kwik-set Jelly.' He circled the kitchen, waving his arms. 'Kwik-set Jelly! Kwik-set Jelly! Where do

I find the Kwik-set Jelly?!'

'Calm down, clammy-pants – you're running around like a headless wombat!' Coco snatched a packet from the cupboard and ran out into the hall again. 'Here you are, Mrs D!'

'Oh, Coco – you've saved my life! I can't make a carriage for a fairy princess without my Kwik-set Jelly!'

'**OOAOWAAAARGHH**!'

No! thought Jack. *Not Margot again.*

'Golly!' said Mum. 'What was that?'

'It's just Mr D in the bathroom,' said Coco. 'Too much gas, apparently.'

'That doesn't sound very healthy,' said Mum. 'I'll ask the doctor to pop up and see him. I'm sure he wouldn't mind.'

Jack peeked round the kitchen door: 'Coco!' he hissed. 'Stop her!'

But now Dr Spleen was coming through the door with his big black bag in his hand.

'**OOAOWAAAARGHH**!'

The doctor raised an eyebrow. He looked up the stairs and stroked his chin. He smiled to himself and nodded, and up the stairs he went, one soft step after another.

'OK, you lot – we've gotta get out of here before Dr Spleen comes back down.' Jack yanked the front door open. He slammed it shut again.

'What's the problem now?' said Coco.

'Mum!' cried Jack, hopping from foot to foot. 'She's waiting in the car! We're trapped, Coco! We can't take Trigger out of the house – she's sitting right outside.'

'Hmm . . .' Coco opened the front door a crack. 'She's busy doing her lipstick. I think we'll be OK.'

Jack peeked out on to the street: Mum was pouting at the rear view mirror. 'Quick,' he said. 'Let's go!'

A curtain twitched in number twenty-eight, as Betty led Trigger through the front door. She paused to nibble at the rose bush.

'Yes, siree!' said Betty, breathing the morning air deep into his lungs. 'The bluebirds are singin' and the honeybees are buzzin'. It's one mighty fine day for a stroll.'

'Come on, come on, come on!' said Jack.

Betty strode out on to Quarantine Street, leading Trigger by her rein. **Clop-clippity-clip** – over the road they went. Jack checked over his shoulder: Mum was fiddling with her tiara. **Clop-clippity-clip** – they turned into Vaccine Lane. Trigger stopped by a lamppost to graze on a clump of grass that was sprouting up through the pavement.

'I've never ridden a camel before,' said Coco. 'Oh, this is gonna be so much fun.'

'Huh?' Jack looked up at Trigger and

swallowed: a string of green drool was dangling off her lip. 'W–what d'you mean?'

'How else are we s'posed to get there?' she said. 'We haven't got time to walk.'

'Haaaaarrrk!'

Jack spun around and clapped his hand to his forehead. 'We forgot Pablo!'

A small black figure with a green tummy was scuttling across the street. 'Hukka-hukka-hukka!' He hopped on to the pavement and pointed his wing at the house.

'Quick,' said Jack. 'Open your backpack, Coco!'

'Haaarrrk!' squawked Pablo, jumping up and down. 'Haaaaaaark!'

Jack scooped him up, wriggling and screeching, and stuffed him in inside.

FIFTEEN

'Y'all ready?' called Betty over his shoulder.

Trigger snorted.

'Wahey!' yelled Coco.

Jack was perched behind her, clinging on to her backpack.

'Let's hit that road,' said Betty, tugging at her reins. 'Giddy up, Trigger!'

Clop-clip-clop – she swayed down Vaccine Lane.

Jack clamped his legs around her belly. Her bristles were grating his ankles as he joggled up and down. 'Hurry!' he cried. 'We've got nine minutes till Lord Crumble lands.'

'Take it easy,' said Betty. 'Like I always says, better slow an' steady in the right direction than a-gallopin' down the wrong track.' He tilted his hat back. 'Now, where's this hoe-down anyways?'

Clip-clip, clippity-clop – Trigger turned off Enema Gardens and into the High Street. A man and a woman on the pavement nudged each other and gawped.

Six minutes, thought Jack. *We've got six minutes.*

Clippity-clip – past the bus stop they went, past Snippets hair salon, the Yummy Tummy Cafe on the corner and the Bun in the Oven bakery.

'Stop!' Jack yelled. 'The traffic light's red.'

'Whoa there, Trigger!' Betty yanked at the reins and the camel jerked to a halt at the junction.

A white van pulled up beside them. Betty looked down at it and scratched his head.

Oh no! thought Jack, as Betty leaned over and rapped on the roof. *What's he doing?*

The driver wound down his window.

'Hey, mister,' said Betty, tipping his hat. 'I'd put a horse on that there wagon if I were you, elsewise you ain't goin' nowheres.'

'You what?' said the man.

'No, siree,' said Betty. 'A wagon without a horse ain't nothin' but a shack.'

The driver looked at Trigger. He wound his window up again.

'Reckon he's gotta few beans missin',' said Betty, tapping the side of his head. 'He couldn't hit a bull with a fistful of banjos.'

Beep-beep-beep! The car behind started honking.

'Move!' called Jack. 'The traffic light's turned green.'

'Quit yer hollerin'!' said Betty. 'You's be a-giving me a sore ear.' He clicked his tongue and Trigger sashayed forward. 'Ya see that?' He nodded at the bank across the road. 'They need to fix some bars on them windows and a padlock at that door, else they'll have One-Eyed Bill a-calling with his shotgun. Why, I remember a hold-up down in Buffalo County –'

'Over there!' Jack pointed to the grocer's on the corner. 'Food For Thought – the shop with the yellow sign.'

Betty tugged his right hand and steered Trigger towards the kerb.

Jack glanced up at the clock tower over the road: sixteen minutes past ten. He hoiked his right leg over Trigger's hump and slithered down her side. 'One minute till landing, Coco – have you got the lollipop ready?'

'Yep,' said Coco. 'Just gimme two seconds.' She shuffled off her backpack, plonked Pablo on the pavement and dug around inside.

'He'll be coming from a south-westerly direction,' said Jack, pointing up at the sky. 'And he'll be landing round about here.' He indicated the spot on the pavement with his toe. 'When I give the signal I want you to –'

'Hold on.' Coco squinted into her backpack and frowned. She rummaged around some more. 'I can't find it.'

'What?' said Jack. 'Are you *sure*? It's gotta be in there somewhere, Coco – have another look.'

She shook her head. 'Nope,' she said.

'It's definitely not here. I reckon I must've eaten it.'

'Tell me you're joking!' Jack croaked. 'Lord Crumble's gonna arrive any second now. *Bam!* Right here on the pavement. And the door will fly open and –'

'Haaark!' Pablo flung his wings in the air.

'Relax,' said Coco. 'I've had an idea. We'll draw a great big trampoline and send him back into space again.'

'Too risky,' said Jack. 'It's hard to say which way he'll bounce, but there's a very good chance he'll get caught in a thermal and end up in Ichihara. There has to be another way.' He paced up and down. *Think, think, think!* 'I've got it!' he cried.

'We'll borrow Betty's lasso! We'll sling it over the Port-a-Lav and pull it really tight.'

'Sounds good to me,' said Coco. 'Except there's one problem — Betty isn't here.'

'Huh?' said Jack. 'I — I don't believe it! Where's he gone?'

The door of the grocery shop swung open and out Betty swaggered, twirling a banana in each hand.

'Well, look-ee here! I just bin and got me a fine pair of pistols.'

'Listen,' said Jack. 'This is an emergency, Betty. We need you to use your –'

'Hey there, mister!' Betty yelled. 'What ya doin' to ma horse?'

Jack turned around: a traffic warden was slapping a parking ticket on Trigger's rear.

'I already told ya once,' said Betty. 'Git your hands off ma mustang, you two-bit rustlin' lowlife!'

'Didn't you read the sign?' said the warden. 'No parking in the High Street between the hours of 9 a.m. and 2 p.m.'

'Betty, *please*,' said Jack. 'Just leave it. We've got a crisis situation and –'

'Ha!' Betty thrust the bananas into his holsters and tore the ticket off Trigger. 'Y'know how horses are, mister? They get kinda hungry this time a day.'

'Don't you get it?' Jack wailed. 'The Port-a-Lav's landing any second and –'

'Zip your lip and hush your tongue. I got a horse to feed.' Betty dangled the plastic envelope in front of Trigger's nose: the yellow teeth opened, a long pink tongue reached out, and the parking ticket disappeared. He dusted off his hands. 'I'm listenin', Erjack – now what was ya hollerin' for?'

'Might as well forget it,' said Coco. 'I don't think Lord Crumble's coming.'

'Of course he's coming,' said Jack.

'I've worked it all out. I've done the calculations.'

'You must've got your sums wrong,' said Coco. 'It's nearly twenty-five past.'

'Impossible!' said Jack. 'And if you don't believe me, I'll prove it.' He counted it out on his fingers again. 'One circuit of the globe . . . a thousand miles an hour . . . turbulence . . . Matterhorn . . . angle of trajectory . . .' He squinted up at the sky. *Uh–oh,* he thought. *I forgot the wind-chill factor. I'll have to make an adjustment.*

Jack coughed. 'OK folks, emergency's over. Lord Crumble's not landing till tomorrow evening, round about quarter to nine.'

SIXTEEN

'Betty!' Jack cried. 'Stop!'

'Whoa, there!' Betty tugged at the reins, and Trigger shuddered to a halt. 'What's a-troublin' you, Erjack? Desperados on the trail?'

'Kelly-Ann – over there! D'you see her?' Jack pointed up the drive: she was holding her clipboard, checking her watch and looking this way and that. He swung his leg over and scrambled down to the ground. 'We'll have to leave Trigger here.'

'Leave her?' said Betty. 'In this here thicket?'

'Yep!' Jack grabbed her reins and

looped them round the branch of a tree
– over and under and round again, in
a triple fishermen's knot. 'In this here
thicket.'

Betty sighed. He heaved his leg over
Trigger's hump and fell on to the grass
with a thud. 'This just don't feel right.'
He picked himself up and shook his
head. 'A cowboy don't never abandon
his horse.'

'She'll be fine,' said Coco. 'See?'

Trigger swished her tail and snapped a
small branch off the tree.

'I guess . . .' said Betty, his voice
trembling. 'But I sure am gonna miss her.'
He sniffled and wiped his runny nose on
the back of his sleeve.

'And that's another thing,' said Jack. 'You gotta start behaving properly. This is the final, remember? And you're the judge.'

'Seems like I can't do nothing right.' Betty looked at the ground and kicked at some leaves. 'Sometimes I get to thinkin' I don't belong around here. Maybes I don't belong anywheres. Ain't come from nowhere, ain't goin' nowhere, an' I sure don't fit in round these parts.' He gave a deep sigh. 'I guess I just ain't cut out for this whole judging shaboodle.'

'Cheer up,' said Coco. 'You can do it, no probs. You just need to act like you own the place.'

'But I'm just a simple cowpoke,' said

Betty. 'I live out on the range an' I sleep under the twinklin' stars. I ain't got no fancy airs and graces.'

'OK. Lemme think . . .' said Coco, twizzling her pigtail. 'Yaks and vegetables. You could try talking about those.'

Betty rubbed his chin. 'Yaks . . . ?' he murmured. 'And vegetables?'

Pablo popped out of Coco's backpack and nodded. 'Huk-huk!'

'OK,' said Jack. 'Everyone ready? 'Cos Kelly-Ann's waiting and I think we should –'

'And you need to shout,' said Coco. 'Like this.' She stamped her foot. '*Hooligan! Pipsqueak! Puffed-up popinjay!*'

'That don't seem so hard,' said Betty. 'I guess I could give it a try.'

'Come on,' said Jack. 'The Cake-Off's started and we've got to –'

'And do a lot of this,' said Coco, waving her arms in the air. '*Who the devil are you?*' she yelled. '*I'll set the peacocks on you and toss you into the blinkin' dungeons!'*

'Haark!' screeched Pablo, flapping his wings.

'Will you lot stop messing about?' Jack cried. 'How many times do I have to tell you? WE – HAVE – TO – GO.'

Coco rolled her eyes. 'Don't get your tonsils in a tangle – I'm only trying to help.'

'So long, partner.' Betty wrapped his arms around Trigger's neck. 'These folks say I gotta leave you here.' He buried his face in her matted orange fur. 'You be safe now. I'll be back before sundown, ya hear?'

A fly settled on Trigger's nose. She closed her eyes and snorted happily.

'Where have you been?' said Kelly-Ann, tapping her watch. 'The contestants have already started.'

'Who the devil are you?' yelled Betty.

Kelly-Ann closed her eyes. 'Count to three,' she muttered. She paused for a moment, then she opened them again. 'Let's get one thing straight,' she said, jabbing at Betty's chest. 'No more funny business.' And she spun on her heel and stalked into the tent.

'Hoo-ee!' Betty slapped his thigh. 'I just love it when a lady talks mean. Lead me to them vegetables, ma'am!'

SEVENTEEN

Jack bumped and shuffled his way along the row till he reached the end and sat down.

Coco turned to him and beamed. 'Oh, I hope your mum wins. She can take us out to Pizza Palace in her new stretch limo to celebrate.' She shivered all over and rubbed her arms. 'I can't wait! I'm getting goose pimples just thinking about it.'

'I dunno,' said Jack, shaking his head. 'I've got a bad feeling about this.'

'There she is!' Coco giggled. 'I think she's in a bit of a tizzy.'

Mum was standing at her baking station, with Kelly-Ann beside her. There were pots and pans strewn across the counter: some were upside down and others were on their sides. Kelly-Ann tapped her microphone. She patted her hair and licked her teeth.

'Ladies and gentlemen, please put your hands together and give a very warm welcome to our first finalist in this year's Cake-Off Competition – Mrs Dorothy Dash!'

Everyone clapped as Mum's face filled the screen.

Yep, thought Jack. *She's in a tizzy, all right.* There was flour on her hands and all over her face, dusting her hair and clinging to her eyebrows. Her tiara was crooked on her powdery forehead.

'Afternoon, ma'am.' Betty clasped his Stetson to his chest and gave a deep bow.

'Lord Stumble!' Mum gasped. She bobbed a curtsey.

'See?' said Coco. 'Betty's doing great.' She gazed into the distance with a faraway look in her eyes. 'I think I'll order the Hawaiian special, and a plate of chips for Pablo.'

'What ya cookin', you frightful pipsqueak?' said Betty, dipping his finger into Mum's mixing bowl.

Mum dusted the flour from her cheek. 'It's a peanut-butter fairy princess cake.' She blinked and gazed into her bowl. 'She was meant to be sitting in a glass carriage.' She shook her head in a cloud of flour. 'I don't understand it! I've looked everywhere but I've lost my Kwik-set Jelly again.'

'Your Kwik-set Jelly's gone a-missin'?' said Betty. 'Ya think some kinda low-down parsnip thieved it?' He rolled up his sleeves. 'Why, if I find that puffed-up popinjay, I'll –'

'Goodness, what fun!' said Kelly-Ann, wrenching Betty away by the arm. 'Let's chat to the other finalists, shall we?'

'Hmm . . .' said Coco. She narrowed her eyes. 'That's weird. I gave her the jelly this morning. I put it in her hand.'

'Huk!' went her backpack. 'Huk-huk-huk!'

The lady in the yellow straw hat turned around and stared.

'You need to keep Pablo under control,' Jack whispered. 'If anyone sees him, we're done for. He's lost his disguise, remember?'

'I've never been in a limo before,' said Coco. 'Bagsy going in the front.'

'Coco? Are you listening? I said –'

'Look!' She nudged Jack with her elbow and nodded at the screen. 'That's Miss Index – she's the librarian at school!'

The audience was clapping. Kelly-Ann was smiling. Miss Index was polishing her spoons. Her pans shone in orderly stacks and her implements lay in neat rows.

'Hoo-ee!' Betty leaned over her

counter and sniffed. 'Smells finer than a yak's backside.'

Jack squirmed in his seat and moaned out loud. *Betty's worse than ever.* And then he heard a rip. *What was that?* Jack stiffened. Just in front of him, an orange tufted muzzle was poking through a tear in the tent.

Trigger? But . . . but I tied her to the tree! Sit still, he told himself, *and maybe she'll go away.*

Trigger curled her lip up.

Jack felt his cheeks go hot. He felt his neck go cold. He heard the canvas rip again as she pushed her neck through the hole, baring her yellow teeth. He reached out his hand to stop her. Too late! She'd clamped her mouth round the brim of the lady in front's hat.

This is bad, he thought. *This is worse than bad – it's cataclysmic.*

With a twist of her head, Trigger whisked the hat off the lady's head. Jack held his breath as it disappeared through the hole. He breathed out again. *Phew! She hasn't noticed.*

'Did you hear that?' said Coco. 'Miss Index is making a liquorice-flavoured laptop with a —' Her eyes widened and she pointed at the screen. 'Yeurgh — there's Dr Purple-Lips!'

Dr Spleen was leering at the camera.

The lady in front was patting her head.

Coco's backpack squawked again.

'And what's our final contestant making?' said Kelly-Ann.

The doctor ran his tongue over his teeth and twisted his pale hands.

The lady in front was looking under her chair.

'Isn't that exciting?' said Kelly-Ann. 'The doctor's planning a little surprise.'

'CONTESTANTS, YOU HAVE THIRTY MINUTES REMAINING!'

Jack could see his mum on the screen. She peered into the oven and bit her lip, then glanced at Miss Index, who was busy with her piping bag.

'Huk-huk-huk!' Coco's backpack was bulging and squirming.

The lady in front turned around again; she stared at Coco and raised an eyebrow.

'I thought I told you to keep him under control,' Jack whispered.

'He's getting all fidgety,' said Coco.

'Something's not right.'

Snap! went the drawstring and the flap flipped back. Pablo popped out of her backpack and pointed his wing at the screen.

'What d'you think you're doing?' Jack hissed. 'Get back in the bag, you birdbrain!'

Coco sat up. She was shaking Jack by the shoulder. 'Dr Spleen! Did you see him? He was fiddling with your mum's oven.'

'The doctor?' said Jack. 'No way.'

'I saw him, you dumb-bum – he was twisting the dial! I knew it!' she cried. 'And I bet he took the Kwik-set Jelly too.'

'Will you two *please* be quiet?' said the lady in front. She stared at Pablo, and her mouth dropped open. 'Norman!' She was jabbing her husband. 'There's . . . there's a penguin in that girl's backpack!'

Coco stood up. She pointed at the screen. 'He's cheating!' she yelled, her pigtails stiff with rage. 'Dr Spleen – he's been cheating all along!'

Jack yelped and yanked at her sleeve.

'Sit down, you freckle-faced fanatic!'

'And let him get away with it? You must be joking.'

'Well, *really*!' tutted the lady.

Jack could feel the knot in his tummy again, and it was twisting tighter than ever. 'Coco, *please* – everybody's staring.' He gave out a squawk. 'Someone's coming over.'

A man in a headset was rushing towards them; he pointed his finger at Coco. 'You! We're filming. Be quiet or leave.'

She stamped her foot. 'Never!'

The man in the headset was easing down the row. He grabbed her by the collar.

'She didn't mean it!' said Jack. 'She's

just a bit upset, that's all – her gerbil's got the chicken-pox.'

'Just you wait!' cried Coco, as the man hauled her outside. 'You'll be sorry! I've got a feather in my backpack and I'm not afraid to use it.'

'See?' said the lady. 'A penguin! It's sticking out of her bag!'

EIGHTEEN

Jack crossed his legs. He clenched his hands. He gripped the side of his chair. His mind was whirling and twisting like a plastic bag in a storm: *The Fruitcake's got my magic feather.* He glanced at the tear in the tent. *She could be drawing anything out there. A catapult or a battering ram or . . . or a suitcase full of scorpions!*

the tannoy sounded. *CONTESTANTS, YOU HAVE FIVE MINUTES REMAINING!*

Jack sat up. Dr Spleen and Miss Index were standing side by side at the presentation table.

Miss Index smiled. On the table before her lay a liquorice laptop, its screen iced with roads and rivers and buildings, and parks dotted with bright green trees.

Dr Spleen smiled. In front of him rose a metre-high dome of clear jelly on a rhubarb biscuit base, encased in a sugar-spun cage. A sugar-spun cage with a bird inside it.

Kelly-Ann glanced down at her clipboard. She made two ticks on the form. She checked her watch and pursed her lips.

Come on, Mum – get a move on! Jack turned to look at the baking area: she was peering through her oven door, wafting her hand.

'Isn't the doctor clever?' said the lady in front. 'That bird's actually moving!'

Moving? Jack swivelled back round and stared at the jelly.

'Must be some sort of clockwork mechanism,' said Norman.

Jack could feel a shiver creeping from the tips of his toes and up his spinal column. *That's not clockwork,* he thought. He rubbed his eyes and looked again. *No, no, no. It can't be.*

It was Margot.

She was trapped behind the sugar bars, inside the jelly dome, her beak open, her wings flapping and her eyes round with terror.

Jack stood up, his heart pounding. *Gotta do something. Gotta do something. Gotta do something.*

'Ladies and gentlemen!' said Kelly-Ann, flashing her smile. 'It's the moment we've all been waiting for – the judging of the Cake-Off final!'

Jack stumbled along the row. He staggered towards the presentation table but the man in the headset was blocking his way. Jack swerved to the left.

He could smell burning.

Mum! He was sprinting towards the baking area now – in, out, in, out – dodging round the stations. He skidded to a stop, his heart thudding. A cloud of black smoke hung over her counter.

'Jack?'

'*Coco?*' He waved at the smoke with his hand. She was crouching on the floor. 'I – I found Margot,' he gasped. 'And she's . . . *Mum?*'

Mrs Dash was curled in a ball beside her. 'Ruined!' she wailed. 'Why? Why? Why?'

'See?' said Coco. 'Now d'you believe me?' She pointed through the smoke to Mum's oven: it was rattling and clanking and hissing.'Dr Spleen's spoiled everything. We're never gonna go to Pizza Palace now.'

'So there you are!' Kelly-Ann Caraway said, leaning over the counter. 'Mrs Dash, didn't you hear? Time's up.'

Mum gave out a whimper.

Kelly-Ann waved at the smoke with her clipboard and coughed. 'Everybody's waiting, Mrs Dash. Why don't you come and show them what a lovely cake you've made?'

Mum shook her head and howled.

'The cameras are rolling, Mrs Dash,'

she said. 'If you don't get up, you'll be letting the competition down, you'll be letting the audience down and, what's more, you'll be letting yourself down. NOW GET UP OFF THE STINKING FLOOR, AND TAKE THAT STUPID TIARA WITH YOU!!!!'

There came a shriek from the other end of the tent.

Kelly-Ann spun around.

'Over there!' cried the lady, waving her finger. 'Runaway penguin!'

A small dark figure was streaking towards the presentation table on a blur of orange feet.

No, no, no! Jack lumbered towards him. *Gotta hide Pablo – gotta hide Pablo!*

'Haaaaaark!' Pablo tugged at the tablecloth and – SPLAT! Dr Spleen's cake toppled to the ground. Pablo's wings were whirring, his beak was pecking, and dollops of jelly and fragments of sponge were flying through the air.

'**OOAOWAAAARGHH**!'

The audience gasped.

Someone yelled, 'It's alive!'

Margot spluttered. She arched her neck and shook out her plumage. She gazed at Pablo and wrapped her wings around him.

Wait! thought Jack. *What's happened to Dr Spleen?*

His black bag was on the presentation table and his white coat was folded beside it, with his stethoscope coiled on top.

'He's vanished!' said Jack.

'Don't worry,' said Coco. 'He's not going anywhere. Pablo pecked a hole in his tyre after we got thrown out.'

'What the blazes is going on?' someone bellowed across the tent.

Every head in the audience turned.

An old man in a battered hat was standing in the entrance to the tent, swaying. His trousers were ragged and scorched, his hair was frizzy and charred, his face was streaked with mud. In his arms he carried a twisted jumble of pipes, which had once been a trombone.

NINETEEN

'What have you done to me peahen?' Lord Crumble cried, pointing a trembling finger at Jack. 'Yes, you!' he spluttered, stumbling through the tent. He turned to look at Coco. 'You and your redheaded accomplice! And there's a third one somewhere. Green pom-pom. Pointy nose. Swedish.'

W-what's he doing here? thought Jack. *He's s'posed to be landing at 8.45 tomorrow evening.*

Lord Crumble was striding towards him now, his eyeballs bulging out of their sockets like a pair of hard-boiled eggs. 'Thought you could get rid of me that easily, eh?'

Jack felt his knees buckle. He grabbed Coco's arm to steady himself.

Up stepped Kelly-Ann. 'Excuse me, this is a ticket-only event.' She looked Lord Crumble up and down. 'With a strict dress code.'

'Quiet!' he barked. 'Or I'll have you strung up by your ankles. Well?' He jabbed at Jack with the end of the twisted trombone. 'Yes, you – you young whelp! What have you got to say for yourself?'

'Um . . . Er . . .'

'Um and er? Is that it? Is that what you and your fellow hoodlums said when you sent me flying into the next parish? I've been upside down in that infernal lavatory for the past twenty-four hours, halfway up a beech tree.'

'Now, see here!' Betty came swaggering towards him, his thumbs hooked into his trousers. He stood before Lord Crumble, his jaw twitching. 'I don't care for the way you're talkin' to ma friends.'

'What are you blethering on about, man?'

'I suggest ya saddle up an' ride outta town,' said Betty. 'And then keep on ridin' till you cross the county line.'

'How dare you, sir,' spat Lord Crumble. 'I *own* this county. And what the devil are you doing in it, anyway?'

'Me?' Betty stretched himself to his full height. 'Why, I just happen to be the judge of this here Cake-Off.'

This is it. Jack swallowed. *They've found us out.* He could feel his face turning numb.

'*You?*' spluttered Lord Crumble. 'Don't make me spit out me dentures. I, sir, am Lord Percy Tankred Witherspoon Crumble. *I* am the Curtly Ambrose Cake-Off judge. Who the devil are you?'

The audience gasped.

'*Him?*' someone whispered. '*Never!*'

Kelly-Ann stepped between them. 'Now, now, gentlemen – I know you're enjoying yourselves, but we don't have time for party games.'

'The name's Crocker,' said Betty. 'Betty Crocker. Fastest gun in Curtly Ambrose.'

Lord Crumble raised the twisted remains of the trombone to his shoulder.

'Let me tell you this, you bow-legged buffoon: I've got a blunderbuss here. It's not pretty, but by gum it's effective!'

Betty whisked the bananas from their holsters and pointed them at Lord Crumble. 'I'm a-warnin' you,' he growled. 'They don't call me Dead-Eye Betty for nothin'.' He took a step forwards. 'Now, I suggest you drop ya weapon, mister, turn ya back and go about ya business.'

'Mister? You *dare* to call me *mister*?' Lord Crumble jabbed the trombone at Betty. 'You'll address me as Your Lordship, or you'll get four ounces of lead shot up yer nostril!'

BANG!!!!!

tWENtY

Jack blinked. His head was throbbing. His chest was heaving. He could hear birds squawking somewhere above him, and the **dong-dong-dong** of the bell in the clock tower, more than a mile away. Slowly, shakily, he picked himself up off the floor. Lord Crumble was standing in the middle of the tent, still clutching his trombone, with Betty facing him, bananas at the ready. Everybody else was lying on the ground.

'C-Coco?' he croaked. 'What just happened?'

'Your mum's peanut-butter fairy princess cake . . .' She was crouching on her hands and knees, staring up at the tent. 'It shot right through the roof.'

Jack looked up at the blackened hole in the canvas: he could see blue on the other side. A crow was spinning in the sky.

'Well!' said Kelly-Ann, scrambling to her feet. 'Wasn't that fun, ladies and gentlemen?' Her teeth were smeared with lipstick and hair was hanging over one eye. She snatched up her microphone from the presentation table. 'Now, I do believe it's time to announce the winner of –'

'Haaaaaarrrk!' Pablo bristled his feathers and pointed his beak at the entrance.

'**OOAOWAAAARGHH**!' screeched Margot. Trigger came lolloping into the tent, flaring her nostrils and whisking her tail.

'W-what's going on?' said Jack. The ground was trembling beneath his trainers. He could hear the rattle of pots and pans. 'Can you feel it, Coco? I – I think it's an earthquake.'

 Fifty ... sixty ... seventy yaks and more, erupted through the entrance,

kicking and bucking and leaping. The air thrummed with the pounding of hooves as they thundered through the tent like a high-speed train – flattening chairs and trampling tables.

'Yee-haw!' yelled Betty, firing his bananas into the air.

Somebody screamed. The audience dived for cover.

The canvas shook. A tent pole snapped. The yaks burst through the other side of the tent and galloped away across the lawn, dragging the back wall with them.

tWENtY-oNE

The audience was huddled on the lawn. Pablo was nestled under Margot's wing and Kelly-Ann Caraway was dusting down her suit. Behind them, the Cake-Off tent was sagging from its poles in shreds, Trigger nibbling on a strip of canvas. The door of Mum's oven lay smouldering on the grass.

'D'you see that?' Coco pointed to the castle: halfway up – right above a window – a thin trail of smoke was curling out of the stone.

Jack stood on his tiptoes. He could just make out a black lump, embedded in the wall. 'Is that my Mum's cake?'

Coco giggled. 'It's stuck.'

'Wow,' said Jack. 'It's made a massive crack.'

Even as they watched, it was spreading over the wall like a lightning bolt in the sky. One of the turrets was trembling. A block of stone fell from the top and tumbled through the air. – it landed in the moat. A couple more followed. The audience backed away, as a piece of wall the size of a car crumbled like a biscuit.

BOOOOMPH!

It hit the ground in a cloud of grey dust.

The huge stone arch over the entrance shuddered and – *CRACK!* – it split in two.

BOOOOMPH! BOOOOMPH!

The turrets toppled. The side walls buckled. A wave of water from the moat sloshed over the lawn.

'No! No! No!' A stooped figure in a battered hat fell to his knees in front of the rubble, quivering and howling as the last wall fell.

tWENtY-tWO

'Fourteen generations of Crumbles, and it's come to this!' Lord Crumble lay on the sodden lawn, beating the ground with his fists. 'My home,' he sobbed. 'My poor, poor home!' Bit by bit, he heaved himself to his feet. 'Clarabelle!' he cried. 'Cordelia!' And he stumbled away, towards the distant fields, still calling for his yaks.

Jack dug his hands deep into his pockets. He stared at his trainers and shook his head. 'Oh, Coco! What have we done?'

'Don't blame me. You drew the Port-a-Lav.'

Jack closed his eyes for a moment. *She's*

right, he thought. *I did.* He turned to her, his lower lip trembling. 'Lord Crumble's lost everything and it's all my fault.'

Coco beamed. 'Tell you what – why don't you draw him another one?'

'Huh?'

'A castle, you numb-bum. Can't be that hard.'

Draw another castle . . . Can I actually do it?

'D'you know something, Coco? I'm gonna give it a try.' Jack reached into her backpack and pulled out the notebook. He smoothed it on to his knee. 'I'm ready,' he said. 'Pass me my feather.'

Jack took a deep breath. He pressed the nib to the paper. *Concentrate,* he told himself. *You've got one chance, Jack — and you can't afford to blow it.* He filled the page with a rectangle and then he drew an arch. He added a triangle at the top for a turret. And another. And another. He sketched slits for the windows here and there and he added a row of flags.

Coco nodded. 'Not bad.'

'Just you wait,' said Jack. 'It'll be even better than the last one.' He tore the page from the notebook and laid it on the ground. 'Stand back, Coco.'

'Amazing,' said Coco. 'It looks just like it! Shame it's a bit too small.' She bent down and prodded the roof with her finger. 'D'you know something, Jack? I think it's a cake.'

'A *cake*?' Jack gulped.

'Yep,' said Coco, licking her finger. 'That's definitely buttercream icing. You should try adding sherbet next time, to make it a bit more zingy.'

'What's wrong with me?' Jack wailed. 'I must be one slice short of a sandwich. I can't get anything right!'

'It wouldn't have made any difference,' said Coco. 'You'll never make Lord Crumble happy. He's the grumpiest man in the world.'

But he must've been happy once, thought Jack. He gazed at the vast mound of rubble

– the broken beams and the old oak table, a silver gleam from the suit of armour, the edge of a gold frame. He looked at his magic feather. *And maybe, just maybe, I can make him happy again.*

'Hey!' called Coco. 'Where are you going?'

Jack was pounding towards the castle ruins. Gasping and panting, he scrabbled over the stones. *Where is it?* He picked up a pewter cup and let it drop. He stumbled over a broken chair leg. He bashed his knee on the four-poster bed. 'Aha!' He tugged the frame from the wreckage. The painting inside it was ripped down one side. He knelt down and wiped the dust away: a familiar face frowned back at him.

'It's him,' Jack murmured. 'Lord Percy Tankred Witherspoon Crumble.'

He turned his magic feather in his hand, and it sparkled like a jewel.

'Hello there, old turnip!' Lord Crumble was waving as he wandered towards the pile of rubble. 'Were you looking for something?'

Jack squinted up at him through the sunlight. *Did it work?*

'Don't think there's anything here worth keeping,' said Lord Crumble. 'Never was! Gloomy old place. Freezing cold. Always thought it was haunted.' He chuckled and rubbed his palms together. 'Always a bright side, eh? No more heating bills!'

Yes, thought Jack. *He's smiling!*

'I think I'll live in a little caravan,' said

Lord Crumble, pointing to a cedar tree. 'Over there – what d'you think? Just like the old days, eh?'

'Yee-hawww!'

'Hello!' said Lord Crumble. 'Here comes that most peculiar fellow, Mr Crocker. Looks as if he's rounded up my yaks.'

The herd was meandering down the hill, with Betty riding beside them, clinging to Trigger's hump. He tugged at the reins and gave a long, low whistle. The beasts paused. Betty clicked his tongue, and they began to scramble up the castle rubble, leaping and prancing over the stones.

'Howdy!' Betty swung his leg over Trigger's hump and tumbled on to the ground. He rubbed his back, adjusted his Stetson and hauled himself to his feet.

Trigger sniffed at the mound of stones, chewing on a fragment of tapestry.

'Well, well, well, Mr Crocker,' said Lord Crumble. 'You've certainly got a way with me yaks. Mountain creatures, you know. Don't like pasture at all. They'll be as happy as sand martins here. I'd offer you a cup of tea but . . .'

'Mighty pleased to oblige, Lord Crumble,' said Betty, tipping his Stetson.

'No, my dear fellow – you must call me Percy.'

'Now,' said Betty, 'seein' as them yaks are settled on that there mountain, I was gonna step over yonder, light me a campfire an' cook me up a mess o' beans. Care to join me, Percy?'

'Beans? I don't think I've eaten beans since I was in nappies. Delighted, my dear chap.'

'Yes siree!' said Betty. 'I reckon me and Trigger will be stayin' here a-whiles.'

As they walked away, Lord Crumble put his arm round Betty's shoulder and began to sing.

'Well?' said Coco. 'What did you draw?'

Jack eased the portrait upright and balanced it on a chunk of stone.

Coco twizzled her pigtail and pursed

her lips. She leaned forwards. Her eyes widened. 'Wow,' she said. 'That's genius.'

Jack nodded. 'I know.' He laid the portrait down again and dusted off his hands. Over the mouth, drawn in scratchy black ink, was a smile. 'Come on,' he said. 'Let's go home.'

Coco pointed to a speck in the sky, which was hurtling towards the horizon.

'There he goes . . .' she murmured.

'Who?' said Jack. 'What are you talking about, you fruitcake?'

'Dr Spleen. Didn't I tell you? I drew him one of your box of biscuits and left it by his car.'

tWEN†Y-†HREE

Jack reached for the doorbell.

Cock-a-doodle doo!

The front door flew open.

'Isn't it exciting?' Mum was beaming. Her tiara was askew on her forehead. 'I've just had a phone call.' She clasped her hands together and did a little twirl. 'I've sold the recipe for my peanut-butter fairy princess cake!'

'Really?' said Jack. 'Are you *sure*?'

'Oh yes! A delightful man rang from Knockdown Demolitions. He was in the audience – he watched it all happen. He says he's never seen anything like it!

Can you believe it? My cake!' She gave a squeak and shivered all over. 'He says it's the hardest material known to mankind. A medium-sized portion could demolish a whole block of flats in under thirty seconds. It'll save him a fortune in dynamite!'

'Well done, Mrs D!' said Coco. 'Maybe we should go out to celebrate.'

'Dotty?' Dad was thumping downstairs, carrying his toolbox. 'I think I found the problem. I drained the system, replaced the stopcock, rebalanced the ball valve, changed the C-valve, double-checked the U-bend and sealed it all with – good grief!' He took off his glasses and rubbed them on his sleeve. 'There's a penguin in the hall.'

Uh-oh! thought Jack. *Pablo's not wearing his disguise!*

'Huk!' Pablo shuffled past Dad and scrabbled up the stairs.

'It must've came in from the garden,' said Mum. 'I saw a cockatoo out there earlier.' She opened the back door.

A palm tree was gently swaying by

the hedge. A pair of humming birds was hovering over a purple hibiscus; butterflies flitted and swooped among the orchids; a bird of paradise was perched in a mango tree with emerald creepers dripping from its branches.

'Goodness!' Dad slid his glasses back up his nose and followed Mum outside. 'They warned me that fertilizer was strong but . . .'

'Hey!' said Coco. 'Where are they going? I thought we were s'posed to be celebrating!' She grabbed Jack's arm and pulled him into the kitchen. 'I'm *starving*. Let's call that stretch limo.'

Jack sighed. 'What stretch limo?'

'The one you're gonna draw.' She

handed him the notepad and pulled out his feather. 'We'll need furry cushions and a fizzy drink dispenser. And don't forget the freezer compartment for the ice creams, and a widescreen TV with a games console. And one of those lava lamps.'

Bump-shuffle-bump!

Pablo was hopping down the stairs again. He had a white handkerchief tied around his neck and a red sock on his head.

'Wowza,' said Coco. 'Looking good, Pablo! All ready for Pizza Palace?'

Pablo waddled down the hall to the front door.

'Hang on,' said Jack. 'The limo's not here yet.'

'Huk-huk!' Pablo stood on the doormat, tapping his orange foot.

'I don't think he's coming to Pizza Palace.' Coco grinned and waggled her eyebrows. 'I think he's going to see Margot.'

Jack pulled the door open. Pablo raised a wing without turning back, and waddled off up the pavement.

'Jack?' Coco prodded him in the shoulder and stared up at the sky. 'Our limo's about to –'

C-C-CLANG!

Jack stumbled sideways, his teeth rattling.

It was straddling the road – a silver-plated vehicle, fifteen metres long. A row of green lights along its side was flashing on and off.

'Are you *sure* that's a stretch limo?' said Coco. She screwed her nose up and frowned. 'It looks more like a runaway train crash.'

'It . . . it's making a funny nose,' Jack whispered.

It was throbbing with a high-pitched hum, like the *twang-twang-twang* of an elastic band.

'Stand back, Coco – it could be dangerous.'

'That's weird.' She peeked in through a side window. 'The seats are glowing.' She turned to Jack, her eyes wide. 'You don't think it's a spaceship, do you?'

Jack gulped. 'Don't be daft.'

'Oooh, look!' She was pointing at the windscreen now. 'It's got a parking ticket.'

'How did that happen? It's only just landed!' He squinted at the envelope on the glass. 'Actually, it looks like a letter.'

Coco beamed. 'Maybe it's an alien message.'

Jack reached out and plucked it from the windscreen. He turned the envelope over, his hearting pounding. He could feel a card inside.

'Oh, I can't wait to see what it says!' said Coco. 'I hope it's written in English.'

Here goes. Jack tore open the envelope and pulled out the card.

'Pablo!' Jack cried. 'Wait!'

On the corner of Vaccine Lane, a little figure turned round.

'We're coming with you!' he called. 'Come on, Coco, let's . . . Coco?'

She was smoothing out her notebook on the roof of the limo.

'What d'you think you're doing?'

'Drawing a driver, of course. Now . . .' she said, turning the magic feather slowly in her hand. 'What do aliens look like?'

ACKNOWLEDGEMENTS

I'd like to thank everyone who helped to make this book: Ben Illis, my agent; Tilda Johnson, who cheerfully edited the mayhem; illustrator extraordinaire, Judy Brown; Robert Snuggs, Valentina Vacchelli, and everyone at Catnip and Bounce, as well as Dr Patricia Brayden and Ravi, who generously shared their medical expertise. My never-ending gratitude goes to Marcus and Milo, for sticking with me all the way.

ABOUT THE AUTHOR:

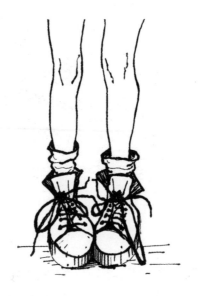

Sophie Plowden is five foot eleven
and three quarters.

She likes painting and writing
and teaching art. And salted liquorice.

ABOUT THE ILLUSTRATOR:

Judy Brown has been drawing pictures
(and writing stories) for as long as
she can remember.

She has three children
and lives in Surrey with her illustrator
husband and two stroppy brown cats.

IF YOU HAD A MAGIC QUILL PEN tHAt MADE ALL YOUR DRAWINGS REAL . . . WHAt WOULD YOU DRAW?

When Jack Dash finds the magic feather, things go from DULL to AWESOME in 0.6 seconds. He can have anything he wants!

Only it turns out Jack isn't very good at drawing . . .
and his life is soon full of unexpected chaos,
frilly knickers and a sea lion.

When he finds himself on the run, it's time for Jack to save the day.
Can he be quick on the draw??

JACK'S SECOND ADVENTURE IS ALSO
WAITING FOR YOU! SPOILER: THERE WILL
BE A SUMMER BLIZZARD!

Jack's friend Coco McBean has stolen it and drawn a penguin
(called Pablo). And the chaos begins…

Giant cupcakes, speedboats, and penguins a plenty – it's up
to Jack to save the day again, but what will he draw?
And why's it snowing in the middle of summer?
And do penguins even eat pizza??

FOR MORE LAUGH OUT LOUD FUNNY BOOKS, FOLLOW THE CAT!

JACK D

AHEM . . . FOLLOW THE **CAT** . . . (*NOT* THE PIG)

www.catnippublishing.co.uk
Twitter: @catnipbooks